Praise for the previous novels of Steve Thayer

Silent Snow

"Thayer uses his mastery of historical detail to build his own spellbinding version of the original [Lindbergh] kidnapping. He also balances the icy clarity of his investigative thinking with the welcome warmth of his characterizations. And in the end, he leaves us with the chilling thought that the snow might never melt on some buried secrets."
—*New York Times Book Review*

"Enticing . . . quirky and complex."   —*Publishers Weekly*

The Weatherman

"A Minnesota thriller with an unpredictable, highly satisfying ending."   —*Washington Post Book World*

"Thayer is a natural storyteller . . . a vital talent."
—*Mystery News*

Saint Mudd

"At once raw-boned and unflinching . . . *Saint Mudd* succeeds."   —*Milwaukee Journal*

"All the roughness and toughness of the best gangster fiction—with a bittersweet ending in the finest tradition."
—Robert Lacey, author of *Little Man: Meyer Lansky and the Gangster Life*

Also by Steve Thayer

SILENT SNOW
THE WEATHERMAN
SAINT MUDD

MOON OVER LAKE ELMO

Steve Thayer

NEW AMERICAN LIBRARY

New American Library
Published by New American Library, a division of
Penguin Putnam Inc., 375 Hudson Street, New York, New York 10014, U.S.A.
Penguin Books Ltd, 27 Wrights Lane, London W8 5TZ, England
Penguin Books Australia Ltd, Ringwood, Victoria, Australia
Penguin Books Canada Ltd, 10 Alcorn Avenue, Toronto, Ontario, Canada M4V 3B2
Penguin Books (N.Z.) Ltd, 182–190 Wairau Road, Auckland 10, New Zealand

Penguin Books Ltd, Registered Offices: Harmondsworth, Middlesex, England

First published by New American Library, a division of Penguin Putnam Inc.

First Printing, July 2001
10 9 8 7 6 5 4 3 2 1

 REGISTERED TRADEMARK—MARCA REGISTRADA

LIBRARY OF CONGRESS CATALOGING-IN-PUBLICATION DATA

Thayer, Steve.
    Moon over Lake Elmo / Steve Thayer.
      p. cm.
    ISBN 0-451-20373-9 (alk. paper)
    1. Minnesota—Fiction. I. Title.
PS3570.H3477 M66 2001

00-066202

Printed in the United States of America

Set in New Caledonia, Times New Roman and Weiss

PUBLISHER'S NOTE
This is a work of fiction. Names, characters, places, and incidents either are the product of the author's imagination or are used fictitiously, and any resemblance to actual persons, living or dead, business establishments, events, or locales is entirely coincidental.

BOOKS ARE AVAILABLE AT QUANTITY DISCOUNTS WHEN USED TO PROMOTE PRODUCTS OR SERVICES. FOR INFORMATION PLEASE WRITE TO PREMIUM MARKETING DIVISION, PENGUIN PUTNAM INC., 375 HUDSON STREET, NEW YORK, NEW YORK 10014.

For Penny
She died like a rose, young and beautiful

PROLOGUE
Zeke—Letter Home
Rejected—Returned to Writer

UNITED STATES NAVY

Feb 5, 1945
Guiuan Samar, Philippines

Dear Folks,

I can't say anything so I'll say How are you? I am fine. And I'm glad you're not here. I doubt this letter will clear navy censors but I want to Rite it anyway. It'll make me feel better. I'll seal it up in a envelope and maybe put a stamp on it and sleep on it I guess.

We shipped out of California on October 26 on board a troop transport. 99 days at sea or so. In December we sailed into Philippines waters. We weren't here long when the Japs showed up. They attacked our ships in suicide planes. Their pilots are called "kamikazes." They have one bomb on the plane and then they fly the plane right into our ships. Our ship got hit right after x mas. We fought the fires hard and tried to get our boys out from the flames but when the sun went down we were still burning and were ordered to abandoned ship. We went over the ropes on the side and into the water and swam for our lives. Another ship was shadowing us just in case. I ripped up my leg going over the ropes but it's going to be OK.

I can't tell you what it feels like to swim through the ocean in the dark while your ship explodes to pieces behind you. I guess all that swimming down at Spirit Lake finally paid off huh.

In the morning we pulled the bodies from the water and counted our dead. Then we wrapped them in canvas shrouds and tied them tight. After a service on deck we committed the boys to the deep. It seemed so unfair just dumping them in the ocean like that but that's what happens when you die at sea. They get no white crosses to mark their graves.

I haven't got any mail yet but I hope to before many more months go by. (A happy thought.) First things first. Yes I got paid. $72.00 but I spent most of it for clothes and such junk. I'm stationed on the southern end of Samar about three miles from a little town called Guiuan. Peace time population about 4500. It's way down on the southern end where the island narrows down to about three miles. Its a long way from Wisconsin any way. Samar is the third largest island in the Philippines. Yes the Japs still hold some of the islands but it's pretty quiet here. It rains a lot. The boys from the Fire Dept. went to chow in a rubber life raft today.

I imagine Dad is home by this time. I'll bet he's got a brand new suit of clothes. Have you heard from Capt. Reggy lately? I got a letter from him in England. He was kind of worried. He's got 250 black boys coming in and he's suppose to train them.

You can imagine how that'll go. Do you think he'll make Major? Big brother is doing OK.

I hear that Bobby Winter was killed when his ship was sunk. I'll bet his mother feels pretty bad about it. I remember the day we all skipped school and inlisted. I'll miss him. Saying a prayer. Amen.

It looks like I'll be out here at least eight or ten months, altho I may be back before that. This point system don't work so good for me. And besides the guys that have the required points aren't going home very fast. You have to have two things to get out. That's 44 points and enough $ to pay someone to get transportation for you to the states. Or you have to be an "officer."

I'm taking progress tests for Seaman 1st class. I don't know whether I'll make it or not. There's quite a few trying for it. It takes a lot of studying. I'm going to do a lot of trying anyway.

I sure would like to be back in good old Birchwood now. I'll bet the snow is getting deep by now. At least enough to track deer any way. Remember that Robert Frost poem about stopping by the woods on a snowy night? We were supos to memorize it. I never did. Wish I had now. Before it slips my mind, will you go and see Mr. Landis and find out how many credits I need to finish high school. And what subjects I need to take. I may be able to finish before I leave this place.

I'll tell you what you can send me. A pen that will write and spell. The summer sausage would be swell. But if you send that, don't send any other food because the taste gets all mixed up. You can send me a book, any kind, something to read.

Well I guess I'd better beat it and get on some dry clothes, it's raining pitchforks and nigger babys. Who knows maybe some day I'll come home.

Zeke

Death ends a life . . . but it does not end a relationship, which struggles on in the survivor's mind . . . toward some resolution, which it never finds.
　　　　　　　　　　—Robert Anderson
　　　　　　　　　　I Never Sang for My Father

1

Angela's Diary

It Is Thursday
April 30, 1992

    The riots began right after the last bell. I ran all
the way home from school so that I could beat Nana's
fifteen-minute deadline and not get in more trouble.
As I was running up the steps all tired out I could
hear the shooting starting. There were clouds of
black smoke from the fires. Miss Crist across the
street yelled at me to get into the house and stay
there. In the house Nana and some of her friends
had the television turned on. Helicopters were
showing the riots. We live up on a hill and my
bedroom is upstairs. It was my mother's room. It is
my favorite place to go. In fact I sleep in the same
bed my mother slept in. So when the sun went down
and it got dark I could see the fires from my bedroom

window. In a really scary way it was kind of pretty. My father told me once that when my mother was just a little girl she watched the Watts riots. It was from the same window. I live in a city where everybody hates everybody. Los Angeles. The city of angels.

There were times I had to stand back from the window because the gunshot noise seemed like it was really close. Some boys from our school ran by and they yelled up at me that they were going to the riots. Big Marvin Sigger was leading them. He's a bully. Everybody at school calls him Sigger the Nigger. My cousin, Raymond, snuck out of the house and went with those boys and he didn't even get in trouble. Raymond is thirteen. He lives with us too because his father committed suicide and his mother was on drugs and didn't want him. Me and Raymond don't get along very well. He picks on me a lot mostly because my father is white. He calls me a little Oreo and a little cracker bitch. I tell him at least my father didn't kill himself. Raymond spends a lot of time at Grandpa's gym hanging around with the boxers. Raymond likes to fight.

Most of the fires that I could see were down on Normandie. That's where all the stores were being looted too. The looters went to Vons and took all the food. Then the looters went to Thrifty Drug Store on the day of their big anniversary sale and cleaned out the place. Nana was really mad about that.

There were no police cars anywhere and Grandpa said if the damn niggers came up the hill we were on

our own. Not even the fire department would come if
they set our house on fire.

Sometimes I'd run downstairs and watch the riots
on television; then I'd run upstairs and watch out the
window. Television was better but the window was
scarier. On television they dragged a truck driver out
of his truck and beat him to a pulp with karate kicks
and bricks. He would have died but some other
people who saw him on television went and dragged
him to safety and took him to the hospital.

In June I will be ten years old. I don't know how
old my mother was when she saw the Watts riots.
Not as old as me, I know. So I think I'm able to
understand it more.

Today was the first day after the riots. There is
still smoke in the air and everybody is angry. Every
once in a while I hear a gunshot and I jump from my
chair. Sigger the Nigger from our school got shot
when he was looting a Korean store. He is in a coma.
I'm really looking forward to getting out of this city
of angels even if I have to die to do it.

This summer I was supposed to go live with my
father in Minnesota until school starts again. Then
Nana said I couldn't go. So I ran away and got
caught.

It would be the first time I've lived with my father
since my mother died. I was just a baby and don't
remember. But my father has told me stories and I
think I can remember Penny holding me. I've been
with Nana and Grandpa ever since she died. My
name is Angela but my father calls me Angel.
Grandpa calls me Stubby because I'm short. Nana

calls me every name imaginable. My father told me
that Penny loved Grandpa very much but that she
couldn't get along with Nana either. Penny moved out
when she was only seventeen.

But now that I tried to run away Nana says that I
can't go anywhere. Especially not Minnesota. That
woman is always trying to mess up my dreams. She
hasn't told my father yet and she won't let me call
him. She took away all of my stamps that my father
bought for me. I thought that if I could just get a
letter to him he would come and get me and
straighten everything out. I was gonna write the
letter last night but then the riots started. That is
why I am so sad and mad and am thinking I'm going
to kill myself. I just don't know how yet. Or when.

Because everybody was watching the riots on
television and Grandpa was standing guard at the
door I didn't have to go to bed last night until really
late. That's when I started having these dark
thoughts. There were gunshots all night long and just
before I finally fell to sleep I was staring up at the
window and I could see the fires from the riots
reflecting off of the glass. I wonder if those are the
flames my mother saw.

2

Steve — Letter to Angela

Jan 1, 1992   Lake Elmo, Minnesota
9:15 P.M.   +7°
Snow Advisory   Windchill −15°

Dear Angela,

Exactly thirty-seven years ago, almost to the hour, my father picked up a pen and began to chronicle the seventy-four days that would cost him his family . . . a daily diary of the last months of his marriage to my mother. I came into possession of it after my stepmother passed away. It is a sad little diary, handwritten on small notebook paper and held together with string. Sometimes it is difficult to read because of his handwriting and his poor spelling, but mostly it is difficult to read because of the things he has to say. But it taught me the importance of leaving behind some kind of written record for your children. So now, with my fortieth birthday in sight, I sit down to this desk and try to put into words my own story for my daughter. I doubt my words will have the power of my father's words. I'm a writer. He worked for a living.

The year was 1944. My father was seventeen years old. He dropped out of high school and joined the navy. Went off to fight in World War II. Thirty years later, I beat the draft, then ran off to Hollywood to be a movie star.

I played football in high school, and two years of college. I was a halfback. Really fast, but a little too small. My jersey number was 22. Anyway, about this time, the war in Vietnam was winding down. To make the drafting of young men more fair, a lottery system was set up. Some clown in Washington would reach into a fishbowl and draw our birthdays. My birthday came up 22. Just like my football number. My friends thought that was really funny. I got a notice in the mail ordering me to report for an induction physical. As I remember it, we were supposed to be called up in June, but the war ended in April, and the draft ended in May. And I didn't have to go.

In my second year of college I was chasing after a girl. Her name was Carolyn. I still have a photograph of her sitting on a suitcase. She wasn't as pretty as your mother (nobody is that pretty) but she was still a beauty. She had round, rosy cheeks with a toothy white smile, and dark brown hair that skirted her shoulders. Of all of the women I never got to date, Carolyn is the one that I regret the most. For a long time I considered her "the one who got away." She took an Introduction to Theater course that year, so I took it because she took it. I was assigned a scene from *Bus Stop* by William Inge. I played the part of the cowboy with the big mouth and the big heart. As I said, Carolyn got away, but I caught the acting bug. My football career ended in the emergency room of Lyon County Hospital. I had a concussion. That means my brain got rattled. By spring quarter, I'd flunked out of college. So, Angel, with little to loose, I ran off to Hollywood to be a movie star.

I packed everything I owned into a 1966 Mustang that I'd bought for six hundred dollars. After a year of the draft hanging over my head, I never felt so free and optimistic in my life. I remember dropping out of the mountains of Utah, and cruising through the California desert in that red Mustang. I remember the scary feeling I had speeding down Hollywood Freeway into the heart of Los Angeles ... a metropolitan area of twelve million people, and I didn't know a soul. No family, and no friends.

In fact, the only thing I knew about theater, I had learned from a book called *Acting Professionally* by Robert Cohen. The book suggested staying at the Hollywood YMCA on North Hudson Street. So after getting checked in at the Y, I slipped on a pair of Foster Grants and went strutting down Hollywood Boulevard in hopes of getting discovered. I mean, I was a good-looking guy, Angel. How long could it take?

There was a movie theater just down the street. Robert Redford was starring in *Jeremiah Johnson*. It was dark when the movie let out, one of those warm California nights. It's a soft warmth we rarely get in Minnesota. I was enjoying the weather and the lights of Sunset Boulevard when a car pulled up to the corner. The man inside leaned over and asked me where I was heading. Said he'd be happy to give me a lift. Now, Angel, my Midwestern brain told me to beware, but my ego was still waiting for Hollywood to discover me. I mean, it had already been six hours. So I got in the car. *Please, don't ever do that.*

He said his name was Fred. Said he was a photographer. I told him I was going to study acting, and that I hoped to break into the movies. He explained how I'd be needing actor's photos. He also said he knew quite a few people in the "business." Boy, was I feeling lucky.

Fred invited me over to his place for a beer. He was a harmless-looking man. Thirtysomething, kind of chubby. We stopped at a liquor store and he picked up a six-pack of Coors. Sixteen-ounce cans. I only mention the size of the cans because, as you know, I don't like beer. Then we drove up to his place in the Hollywood hills.

Fred had a great apartment, with one of those swimming pools out front that glistens in the moonlight, just like in the movies. We sat on his couch and popped open our beers. Fred popped on the television set. It was *Barnaby Jones*, in color . . . starring Buddy Ebsen as Barnaby Jones. So I was sitting there sipping my beer, half watching Buddy Ebsen stagger through his lines, and half listening to Fred talk about the "business." The strange thing was, all the time Fred was talking to me, he kept putting his finger on my leg for emphasis. And I couldn't help but notice that that finger was working its way up my thigh. I guess by then, I should have been suspicious.

There was a break in the action. *Barnaby Jones* went to a commercial. There was also an awkward break in our conversation. Fred just sat there staring at his beer, all deep-in-thought-like. Then suddenly out of the blue, he blurted out, "May I kiss you?"

I couldn't believe what I had just heard. Still, I knew that I had heard it. This grown man wanted to kiss me. I was at his place drinking his beer, and I'm from Minnesota, and I didn't want to seem rude, so I pretended that I was thinking about it. After few frightening seconds, I gulped, and said, "No."

We sat in icy silence, the minutes ticking by. Finally I turned to him and said, "Are you a homosexual?"

Now, I know that you know what a homosexual is, because you wrote and told me . . . though I still doubt a pair of ten-year-old boys can have a homosexual relationship, no matter how queer you say they act. Anyway, things were different when I was your age. We weren't quite as sophisticated. It was 1974, I was twenty years old, and I'd just fallen off the turnip truck from Minnesota. What did I know about homosexuality?

Fred looked at me strange like, then answered my question. "Yes, I am."

I thought about that for a minute, then confessed to him, "You're the first homosexual I've ever met."

Then Fred said to me, and remember these words, Angel, "Well, I won't be the last."

So I had a sixteen-ounce can of Coors that I couldn't drink, I was watching *Barnaby Jones*, which I couldn't stand, and I was sitting next to the first homosexual I'd ever met. I started doing one of those time-to-get-going routines. I yawned. I glanced at my wrist as if to check the time . . . and I didn't even have a watch. At last, I got up the nerve to say, "Well, Fred, it's time I was going."

"I could read your mind," he said.

Fred offered to drive me back, but I insisted on walking . . . it couldn't be more than five miles. I knew the YMCA was near the Capitol Records Building, which is tall, round, and shaped like a stack of records. I could see it in the skyline off to the east. I hurried down the hill to Hollywood Boulevard, and started in that direction. It didn't take

but a few blocks for me to realize what Hollywood Boulevard became after dark. I know they've cleaned it up some,
but back then it was a combat zone. It was one porno theater after another. Sex shops and head shops. There was
nothing on the street but johns and hookers. Pushers and
pimps. I had never seen anything like it. It was fascinating
and frightening at the same time. I was scared. So I walked
a block, then I ran a block, then I walked a block, then I
ran a block. I did this all the way back to the YMCA.

I went to my room and locked the door. It took me a
while to settle down. I turned on the TV. I was listening to
Johnny's monologue when there was a knock at the door. It
was another guy who was staying at the Y. I'd met him earlier in the day. He said he'd seen my light on. Asked if I
wanted some company. He was from Indiana, a fellow Mid-
westerner, so I figured he was safe. And frankly, I did need
someone to talk to.

So we were sitting on this dirty little couch watching *The
Tonight Show*, and I swear, Angel, I was just about ready to
tell Indiana Boy about my traumatic experience in the
Hollywood hills when he leaned over to me and said those
same exact words: "May I kiss you?"

Damned if Fred wasn't right!

I lost my cool. I stood with clenched fists, yelling at him
to get out of my room. He looked scared to death. After
he'd vanished, I locked the door and pushed a dresser up
against it. I checked out of the Y the next morning and went
looking for an apartment. I swore to myself that if I didn't
find my own place by the end of the day, I was leaving L.A.
for good. If I wanted to be an actor, I'd go to New York City.

Yes, that's right, at about the same age my father was
fighting off Japanese war planes in the South Pacific, I was

fighting off homosexuals in Hollywood. Now almost twenty years later, I look back on my first night in Hollywood and figure, what the hey, I wasn't offered any acting jobs, but I was offered two kisses.

Your assignment for the next letter is to look up the words *chronicle* and *induction*.

I love you, Angel. I'm really looking forward to our summer together.

You're going to like it here.

Steve

3

From the Diary
of P.A. Thayer

St. Paul, Minnesota
Jan 1 Sat 1955   *day 1*
8:30 P.M.

An uneventful day. Kate had to go to work at the Idle
Hour at 8 P.M. I don't believe she will enjoy it very much
as she was very tired from working there last nite. Being
New Years eve she had to work almost all nite. I'm a bit
tired myself from the doings of last nite. Well I think I'll
pack Steve off to bed and retire myself. Maybe I can get in
an hour or so of sleep before one of the kids puts up there
nitely howl.

Am looking forward to a good year in which we will
suffice a bit better than last.

It sure was a nice day today. I think the temp got up to
around +32°F. I hope the balance of the winter is mild.

Jimmy is crying. Guess he must have lost his bottle. Think I'll straighten him out and go to bed.

⌒

Jan 5 Wed 1955   *day 5*
10:15 P.M. Temp +22°

Still foggie, but not as frostie as this morning. Just went down to Idle Hour for Kates check. Needed it kind of bad cause the insurance man was here this eve. Work at Swift is slacking off a little each day.

Kate looked all day for another job. Don't look too good. I guess she's going down to Civil Service Comm tomorrow to see if they have anything.

⌒

Jan 6 Thurs 1955   *day 6*
9:05 P.M. Temp 12° above

Today was just another day at Swift.

Kate found a job today. West Publishing Co. Hope she likes it. She starts work Monday at 9 A.M. She starts Proof Reading at $175.00 a month. Had to take a spelling and reading test.

Dad Walker's birthday today. He's 65. Kate, the Kids and I were over there this eve for a while. Ruth & Harv were there too. Fern (babysitter) said I had a caller while I was gone. He asked for Zeke. Can't imagine who it was.

Fuel oil went up to 17¢ Per gal at M & H. (Too high) Enough for tonite.

~

Jan 7 Fri 1955   *day* 7
8:40 P.M.

   Well it was rather a mild day today. +24° Rite now.
Swift layed off 10 men from the Freezer 2nd shift today. A
sure sign of the slack season due shortly. Kate had to go to
work at the Idle Hour again tonite and I guess Sat nite
too. That will come in handy. Didn't get much of a check
today. Think I'll go and see the Personnel man next week
and see if there isn't a better job somewhere for me.
Checks are getting too small in the Freezer.
   Nuff said.

~

Jan 8 Sat 1955   *day* 8
P.M. +24°

   Another nice day. Rather cold this morning tho.
Went to the Salvation Army store and got 2 coats and
1 pair shoes for the kids and a necklace for Kate all
for $1.85.
   Kate went to work at Idle Hour again tonite. Last time
for a while I hope. Think I'll ride the bus next week to
work in an effort to save a little cash. Pretty broke. Mom
said that her and Dad may go to Rice Lake tonite. I
wonder if they went. Dad wanted to see about buying a
house there to live in after they retire.
   Well guess I used enough paper for tonite so that's all.

Jan 11 Tues 1955   *day 11*

Snowed some today. Not bad, but snow anyway. Kind of nice out tho. Just took Kate & Ma Walker down town to play bingo. Hope they win something. We're almost *Broke*.

I sure have been having a rough time at work. Been back on my old job more or less. Lots of livers. Hope it brings our business up a little. It should.

Mom & Dad Walker sold there house today. They've got 30 days to get out. That means we have 30 days to fix up washer to wash clothes at home. That will take some cash we haven't got. But we'll find a way some how.

Think I'll eat the rest of Steve's apple and go to bed and read awhile.

Jan 12 Wed 1955   *day 12*

A lot of snow this A.M. Took 20 minutes to get downtown. Lots of traffic. Washed clothes over at Walkers.

Lots of wet meat at work.

Prediction for tomorrow A.M. −5°.

Jan 13 Thurs 1955   *day 13*
9:40 P.M.

   It was quite cold all day. Just another day at Swift. Tomorrow its pay day which is a good thing. Kate is at work at the Idle Hour again tonite. She started at 8:00. It sure don't give her much rest working 2 Jobs. I don't really know if it pays for her to work or not. Out of $40 odd she gets per week U.S. takes $10. Fern $15. After food, leaves about $8 or $10. Not much for 40 or so hrs work. About the only thing we come out on is her waitress work at the Idle Hour. Its no sin to be *Broke* but it sure is inconvenient!
   Think I'll go to a show tomorrow nite then go down and pick up Kate when she gets off work.
   Sure would like to go to Chicago some weekend again. Just to get away from it all and relax and cool off a bit. Get my news all lined up again. I think Kate would enjoy it too. She'll need a rest before long if she trys to keep up this pace.

Jan 14 Fri 1955   day 14
6:45 A.M. +23°

   Kate got home about 1:30 last nite.
   Eve: Got home from work at usual time had supper and headed for the store. Old Henry stopped right smack in the middle of the Conway St hill, so I backed it down around and to hell with it. Had to walk to store. Came back and walked over to Walkers to get tools and light. Checked points on car to no avail. Bout that time Ruth

and Harvey came along so they took Kate & I downtown.
Kate went to work and I to a show. After show I went and
sat in the Idle Hour and waited for Kate to get out of work
then we went to nite spot and had a small steak each and
took a taxi home and so to bed at 2:00 A.M. Kate was very
tired (me too).

~

Jan 15 Sat 1955   day 15

Got Kate up at 5:30 this A.M. But she was too tired to
go to work so back to bed we went. Got up at 10:30 and
got my car up in the yard with much wheel spinning etc.
Darn thing had a frozen gas line.

Went to Grannies for lunch. When I got home Kate
was sound asleep in preparation for work this eve. Steve &
Jim were taking there naps and Larry and Chris were out
playing in the alley with there sleds etc. Kate sure is
looking rough. I hope she can get some rest Sunday so she
will feel better next week.

Well I suppose I should get Steve ready for bed and
chuck him in for the nite. I'm getting rather tired myself.
This has been a long day for me. I've got to find a way to
make a little extra jingle. I wonder if I could Rite a short
story or something. Should give it a try. I wonder how
much they pay for such things.

4

Steve—Letter to Angela

Jan 4, 1992
11:15 P.M.
−16°

Lake Elmo, Minnesota
New Moon
Windchill −31°

Dear Angela,

It's the coldest night so far this winter. The sky is icy clear and all of the Northern stars are out. I stood in the bay windows and watched the moon come up over Lake Elmo. What a sight it was. Indians call it the New Moon of the Deep Snow. Makes it look like heaven out there. The snow was late in coming this winter, but now it's here in all of its celestial beauty. The pine trees are layered in white, and the farm field across the road is a rolling sheet of unblemished snow that perfectly reflects the moonlight. I wish you could see it, Angel. By the time you get here this summer, it'll look totally different. Pretty, but different.

There's an old Dionne Warwick song that says all the

stars that never were are parking cars or pumping gas. I was parking cars. That's where I met Penny. It was 1979.

I never expected to fall in love with a black woman. If I gave black women much thought at all, it was only because of Diana Ross and The Supremes, or Marilyn McCoo of The 5th Dimension. I grew up in a white city in a white state. I went to a high school with over two thousand students. Only two of them were black. Maybe once a week I'd pass them in the halls.

I'd been in Hollywood for five years and was still making my living as a parking garage attendant at the Boneventure Hotel downtown. I don't think it was love at first sight, but Penny was strikingly beautiful at first sight. She had the thickest head of hair I've ever seen on a woman. She cared for it meticulously. One hour in the morning. One hour in the evening. Think about that, Angel. Two hours a day, 365 days a year. Your mother spent 730 hours a year on her hair. But it was worth every second. When I first saw her in the casket, I made them do her hair over again.

She had one of those hourglass figures. Slender, but shapely. She loved chocolate, but never gained an ounce of weight. Even when she was pregnant with you, there was little weight gain. Of course, we didn't know then that she was already sick.

The thing of it was, I could talk to Penny. This was amazing because our backgrounds could not have been more different. We had nothing in common. She grew up on a hill in the Boyle Heights section of Los Angeles. I grew up on the East Side of St. Paul. The only thing she knew about Minnesota was that it is cold.

"I don't care how many seasons you got, I'd never live anywhere where it snows."

That's what your mother thought of Minnesota.

Penny was the hostess with the mostess. She greeted the dinner crowd arriving in their cars. Wrote them a claim check. Directed them to where they were going. It wasn't much of a job, but she did it well. She looked beautiful out there in her frilly blouse and her dark vest, those long legs in a pair of tight slacks, that big smile on her face. Guys were always hitting on her. Our favorite part of the job was jumping in Corvettes and cruising through the garage. As soon as a Corvette drove through the entrance gate our eyes lit up. We didn't need words. No signals. Penny wrote the driver a claim check, and as soon as he disappeared through the double doors . . . I was behind the wheel and she was climbing in the passenger side. Penny only wished for two things in life: She wanted to own a white Corvette, and she wanted to have lunch at a sidewalk café in Paris.

One day I came to work and as I was signing in Penny said to me, "Steven, take me to a movie."

The pen went flying from my hand. Penny burst out laughing. When one of our coworkers asked what was so funny, I told him the job was starting to get to me . . . I was having fantasies about beautiful black women asking me out on dates. Penny and I had become good friends by then, but I still wasn't sure about dating.

Eventually I got up the nerve to ask her out, but we didn't go to a movie. Instead I took her to the Shubert Theater in Century City to see *Evita*. I told Penny I was taking her to the white part of town because I was worried some of the "soul brothers" would see me with her and beat the hell out of me.

"I'd beat them up," she promised.

After the play we had dinner at an Italian restaurant.

Good wine and good laughs. I bought her a rose. The first of many. Then we made our way back to my dumpy apartment in North Hollywood. I guess if you turned out the lights, the place wasn't that bad. We were slow dancing to a Crystal Gayle song (it was the '70s). A candle was glowing. I was holding her tight when she said, "I can't believe you've never kissed a black girl."

And so for the first time we kissed. It was one of those moments, one of those feelings, almost spiritual, that comes only once in a lifetime. "Can I kiss you again?" I asked.

"Steven, you can kiss me all you want."

I loved the way she always called me Steven. The only other person who called me Steven was my mother, when she was mad at me. Your mother's name was Penny, and nobody dared call her anything else. She was into birth certificates. If that was the name printed on your birth certificate, then that's what she called you. Bobs were called Robert. Jim was James. Steve was Steven. She hated it when I called you Angel instead of Angela. Anyway, Penny and I were seldom apart after that night.

I didn't have much money back then, but I managed to save enough for her wedding ring. And I saw to it that we were married on Catalina Island, off the coast. Just the two of us, a justice of the peace, and some stranger for a witness.

I have a picture of your mother standing at the foot of the bed one night on our honeymoon. I'll show it to you this summer. She's wearing a silvery-white nightgown. Her hands are folded in front of her. Her hair is down. She has a shy smile on her face. She looks like an angel would look. I remember saying that night that if we ever had a daughter we'd name her Angel, after her mother.

The clock in the office just struck two. Enough for to-night. Better check the furnace again, the gas valve got stuck open. Then to bed. Maybe I'll write another page tomorrow.

Jan 8, 1992
11 P.M.

Sorry, Angel. The days slipped by. Red-letter day . . . Jan 8th. My sister's birthday. Day my father died.

Temps still below zero. More snow.

I went down to the Ramsey County courthouse today. Found my parents' divorce records from 1955. It was pretty dry stuff. No surprises. It was uncontested.

Your assignment for next letter is to look up the words *celestial* and *unblemished*.

I love you, Angel. See you in the summer.

Steve

5

Angela's Diary

It Is Saturday
May 2, 1992
And it's smoggy today

Nana is mean sometimes but she only beat me up
that once. It was on Good Friday a few weeks before
the riots, and it was pretty bad. After Grandpa came
and got me at the bus station, Nana was waiting for
me at home. When I was walking up the stairs to the
front door it was like walking to an execution. I could
see her staring at me out the window. She looked
mad as a pistol. With fire in her eyes. I was really
scared. I knew she was going to hit me as soon as I
walked in the door but I didn't expect to get a
beating. My hair is really long and really thick.
People say I have the thickest head of hair they have
ever seen. Nana says I'm vain about my hair. She

says it's white girls' hair. As soon as I got in the
house Nana had her hands in my hair and she was
pulling me around the front room and hitting me at
the same time. Her fingers got caught in my hair and
she didn't even care. She just kept pulling me and
slapping me. There was nobody around to help me.
Raymond was so scared he turned and ran outside.

I begged Nana to stop because my nose was
bleeding and I think my mouth too. She dragged me
over to the stairs and told me to get my ugly green
eyes up to my room and never come out. She was
yelling stuff like, "You think you're better than all of
us, well you ain't!"

I don't think I'm better. I'm just different!

There was blood running all over my school
clothes. Instead of going upstairs like Nana said I
turned and ran outside. I went down the steps as fast
as I could and started running down the hill. But
Nana was chasing me and she caught up with me
down by old lady Miller's house. Then she started
beating on me again really bad. I could see Raymond
and his friends watching from up on the hill but they
were too afraid of Nana to help me. Then Nana was
dragging me home by my hair when Miss Crist
across the street came running out of her house. She
was yelling at Nana to leave me alone. Said she had
called the police. I thought Miss Crist was going to
have a fight with Nana right there on the sidewalk.

The police came later to the house. But they didn't
do anything to Nana because I had tried to run away.

You see I was promised by Grandpa and Nana that
I could go spend the summer with my father in

Minnesota. But then for no reason Nana said, "No
you can't go. I changed my mind." So I ran away.

I took all of my money to school with me and right
after the last bell I took a city bus downtown to the
Greyhound bus station. It was really crowded. There
were long lines at the ticket windows and the
schedules on the boards were impossible to read. The
counters were really tall and I could barely see
inside the ticket windows. I waited until the lines
disappeared. Then I went up to a window that had a
lady working, because she looked nice.

"Where are the buses that go to Minnesota?"

"Minnesota?" she said. "I don't think we have a
bus that goes that far. I think you have to take a bus
to Denver, Colorado, then you can take a bus to
Minnesota. Are you asking for your mother?"

"No, I'm asking for my father. How much would a
ticket cost?"

"All that way would be over a hundred dollars."

Well I didn't have over a hundred dollars. I only
had about seventeen dollars. So I was sitting on a
bench counting my money when a bus driver came
and sat down next to me. He was nice. He had some
gray hair like Grandpa. He had a little bag of potato
chips and he offered to share. I was hungry because
it was past supper already.

"You here all alone?" he asked me.

"Yes," I told him.

"Little girl sitting at a bus station all by herself,
counting her money. Sounds to me like a little girl
trying to run away from home."

"I want to go see my father in Minnesota."

"Well now, that's a nice thought. When I was in the army, long, long time ago, I had a friend from North Minneapolis. He wasn't from Minneapolis, understand, he was from North Minneapolis. Went to North High School. He always made sure he got that 'north' in there. He was a good man."

"My father lives in Lake Elmo. It's by Minneapolis because he drives there to work."

"And what kind of work does your daddy do?"

"He writes news and books."

"That's an important job. And where's your momma?"

"She died when I was a baby. She had sickle-cell anemia."

"I'll bet you live with your grandma then, don't you?"

"Yes."

"And does she know you're at the bus station?"

"No."

"What's your name?"

"Angela."

"Well, Angela, you ain't got enough money for a bus trip all the way to Minnesota. And you can't sit down here all night. Gonna be dark soon. Your grandma, she'll be worrying about you. We'd best call her, OK?"

"Will you call my grandpa instead?"

Grandpa is blind in one eye, so he looks mean. But my grandpa is everything a grandpa should be. I love him very much. He didn't yell at me or nothing that night. We left the bus station and drove home. Grandpa parked in front of the house. Then we just sat there. The sun was going down through the smog and everything in the sky was fuzzy orange like fire.

I told Grandpa, "I just wanted to go see my father."

"If your daddy wanted you with him so bad, he never would have run back to Minnesota in the first place. After Penny died he left here and he never even looked back. It was three years before he started writing. It was five years before he came out here to see his own daughter. He don't know what it means to be a father."

I started crying when he said that.

"Don't get me wrong, Stubby. I like your daddy. He was a good man to your mother. But I don't think he should have run off like that. A man has responsibilities. Least they did when I was growing up."

"Is Nana mad?"

"She's madder than a pistol, Stubby. You're gonna have to take your licks."

"Did Penny fight with Nana?"

"Fight? Those two had a war going. Damn near drove me to drinking. I finally told Penny, if two people can't live together in the same house, one of them has to leave. Your nana would never admit this, but she cried her eyes out the day Penny left the house. You know between me and Nana, and your daddy and you, I sometimes wonder if we're all living in the same world. I'm going down and close up the gym. You go on in the house now."

6

From the Diary
of P.A. Thayer

Jan 16 Sunday 1955   *day 16*

   Brrr. 8:20 P.M. Well it got all the way up to +8° today.
Very warm eh. Old Henry started up very well this morn.
The darn thing still don't run Rite. So here I sit awaiting
Ferns arrival so I can journey after fuel oil.
   Well no let up in our finance situation. How ever
I hope to bring our debts at least up to date in a month
or six weeks. By then spring should have sprung. (I
hope.)
   I sure hope we can get our T.V. fixed soon. Then
I'll have something to do when Kate works at nite.
Altho this little book may suffer somewhat. Well I've
got to go back to the old ice box tomorrow. Got to
bring home the bacon you know. I may freeze my toes
but . . .

Dad now thinks he will move back to Birchwood when he retires. I wonder where it will be tomorrow.

It sure is getting cold out. Hope it warms up. Fuel oil is getting too high. I think it is rather strange that in this day and age of atomic power etc. that we can't have a cheaper fuel in this north country to off set the high cost of heating our homes. It is my opinion that a cheaper way of manufacturing electricity would solve the problem. Perhaps the development of solar power would be the answer. Either individual home units or community plants could be employed. (A thought.)

Just rocked Jim for a while. Didn't do any good he's still awake darn it.

A low of $-5°$ tonite. A high of $+10°$ tomorrow is predicted.

Again I say Brrrr. I'm rather suprised that my bad leg hasn't been acting up on these cold days.

Well Fern just arrived so I guess I'll call an end to this nite.

~

Jan. 17 Mon. 1955   *day 17*
10:45 P.M. I would say it was around 0°.

Kate was a bit late coming home from work tonite. She is putting up her hair in preparation for bed. (don't think I'll bother myself.) Think I'll just dive in.

~

Jan 18 Tues 1955   *day 18*

    Darned old car broke down again today. It is now in a garage in south St. Paul. Had to ride the bus home from work tonite.
    Kate is working again tonite. She don't feel too well.

~

Jan 19 Wed 1955   *day 19*

    Got the car out today. Cost $4.60.
    Kate didn't work. She went down town this after noon but isn't back yet at 6:55.
    2:25 A.M. Rough evening.

~

Jan 20 Thurs 1955   *day 20*

    Snowed last nite several inches. Had a hard time staying awake today. Came home early from work.
    To bed. 11:30

~

Jan 22 Sat 1955   *day 22*

    Kind of chilly out. Kate washed clothes at Walkers. Mom is baking an angel food cake for us for Sun. Got a new fuel pump for Henry today. Didn't install it yet tho. Ruth & Harvey are coming over for diner tomorrow and maybe Les, a fellow Kate and I met down on the corner of 9 & St. Peter. Kate left for work about 8:00 at the Idle Hour.

I finally got all the kids asleep. Just finished the dishes and the bathroom floor. Boy I'm getting dish pan hands. Hope Kate gets home early tonite so she'll feel good tomorrow. I sure love that gal. I'd do any thing for her.

The days are getting a bit longer now. Sun Rise 7:31, set 4:52 today. Well guess I'll drink coffee and retire. Hope kids sleep all nite.

~

Jan 23 Sunday 1955　　　*day* 23

We sure had a good dinner today. Harvey & Ruth were here. Les didn't show up.

Well the temp got clear up to +10°. All the kids are in bed but Steve and he's about tired enough to go any time. Fern isn't back yet but I guess she'll be here around 10. Kate left for work at I.H. at about 8:10. I *may* go down for a few minutes after Fern gets here.

I read a nice little article about Canada. Got me all excited about it. "Go North Young Man." That sort of thing. Darn cold up there tho.

Income tax coming up. Hope we get something back again this year. Guess I'll sign off and go see Kate and get some fuel oil.

Fern just got here. 9:55 P.M.

~

Jan 24 Monday 1955   *day 24*

Kind of cold out. Kate didn't work today. Too tired. I went in late. Strain on lower abdomen hope I get over it soon.

⌒

Jan. 25 Tues 1955   *day 25*

This promises to be a dandy. Bet it winds up −10° before morning. Kate is at work at the Idle Hour again.

That Formosa deal sure looks bad. Glad our boys are too young for service.

I think I'll look for a little gift for Kate. I have something in mind. Perhaps I can get it by valentines Day. Feb 14. Must also get something for Chris. His birthday is Thurs. Jan 27. I think.

Think I'll go to bed shortly altho I don't feel sleepy.

⌒

Jan 27 Thurs 1955   *day 27*

The wind is blowing quite hard. The man on the radio said it will be 15 below zero tonite. I wonder if the Ford will start.

I'm supos to see a Doctor about my trouble today. But my trouble is gone so I think I'll have Swift cancel it for now.

Chris's birthday today. Kate is going down town to get a gift for him and maybe a cake. Les is going to help her.

I'm going to trust his judgment. I believe him to be a fair man. At the present time at least.

Les is the guy who is competing with me for my wife. I'm going to try every angle to keep her with me. However if she decides she no longer wants me and wants him. Then her happiness comes first. (Nuff said.)

7

Steve—Letter to Angela

Jan 12, 1992   Lake Elmo, Minnesota

Dear Angela,

Boy, Angel, is it cold. It's 10 degrees below zero right now and snowing hard. Do you know there are companies here in Minnesota that won't bring new employees to town until springtime. They're afraid if they show up for the first time in January, they'll turn around and go right back where they came from. We have to show people how pretty it is here in the summertime and autumn, then we kind of work them into winter.

My mother and father divorced when I was only two years old. I have no memory of living with my father . . . I guess that runs in the family, huh? When I say "my parents" I'm usually referring to my mother and my stepfather . . . Les. That's who I grew up with, just a few blocks away from the small house on Euclid Street where my real father wrote his diary. I have only scattered memories of living there. I drove by the old place last week after picking up their divorce papers. There's a garage on the property, but the house is gone. It was nothing but a shack for working stiffs.

I was three when we moved into the house on Wilson Avenue. And it was in that house on Wilson that Kate and Les fought like a cat and a dog for twenty years. I can't count the number of things that went flying through the air over the years. A steam iron. A heavy glass cigarette lighter. A butcher knife. They spent one night throwing silver dollars at each other. Funny thing is, there were few injuries. It still amazes me how so many flying objects could miss so many people. The projectile I remember most was the flying Christmas tree, but that's another story for another time.

By the time I was in high school my mother had taken to drinking. Mostly beer. By the time I graduated, she was an alcoholic. I remember her as two different people. She was the president of the Mound Park PTA, an all-American mom who drove the peewee football team from game to game through four sons. In later years she was a drunken lunatic with a violent temper. If you think Nana is bad, you should have seen my mother drunk. Even in her drinking days, she was nice right up until she got some beer in her. The fireworks didn't start until she got home from the bar. Mom had to get drunk to get mad.

Kate and Les used to take turns running away. Us four boys slept in one big bedroom overlooking the street. My half-sister, Mary, was across the hall. My mother's bedroom was next to my sister's, and until the day he died, your grandpa Les, not-so-affectionately known as "the old man," slept on the couch in front of the television set. Don't get me wrong, Angel. I loved my stepfather. I just never liked him.

It was usually late at night. The old man would come into our room and wake us up. He was normally an S.O.B., until it came time to run away. Then he'd tell us what great kids we were, and how proud he was to have raised us. He'd shake hands with each one of us. Said he was going back home to Ohio. Remember, we were still half asleep while this was going on. He'd get into his car, back out of the driveway, and we'd watch as the taillights disappeared up Wilson Avenue, hoping the son of a bitch really had returned to the Buckeye State. Two or three days later, we'd come down for breakfast and the old man would be sitting at the kitchen table with a cup of coffee and the morning paper, as if nothing had happened.

Now when my mother ran away, it was a different story. She would march into our room ranting and raving about what no-good kids we were, always saving her most venomous farewell speech for "Steven." When my first book was published, I couldn't bring myself to put the name *Steven* on the jacket cover because it still reminded me of my mother screaming at me. Not even Penny could rescue the name. Anyway, out the door Mom went, slamming it behind her. She'd get into her car and drive back up to the neighborhood bar on Old Hudson Road.

One night Mom came home from the bar in a drunken rage, burst into our room while we were sleeping, and woke us up with a tirade about why she was leaving us. Then off she went. Apparently, she didn't know that just an hour earlier we had been awakened to shake hands goodbye with the old man. We didn't have any parents for three days. It was probably the most peaceful three days that house on Wilson Avenue had ever known.

It's peaceful here tonight. Winter wonderland. I shoveled snow again today. My back is killing me. I had an afternoon dentist appointment in St. Paul. The roads were terrible. Snow and ice. Traffic was really heavy. I bought the new Bruce Springsteen cassette. Listened to it all the way back to Lake Elmo.

Your assignment for next letter is to look up *tirade* and *venomous*. And *projectile*. Let me know. It's 2:00 A.M. Two aspirin and to bed.

I love you, Angel. See you in the summer.

Steve

8

Angela's Diary

It Is Tuesday
May 5, 1992
<u>Cinco de Mayo</u>

It is near midnight and I am writing under the
covers with the flashlight that Grandpa gave me. I
am pretty depressed. Seems every day I die a little
more. I might not even live to kill myself. After
school it was nice and sunny outside and all my
friends were out playing. And I'm grounded! I even
ran out of homework to do. School will be out for the
summer next month and I should be on my way to
Minnesota. But it don't look like it's gonna happen.
My father once told me that life dealt me a bad hand.
I asked Nana if she had called my father yet to tell
him that I'm not coming. She said she'd call him
when she damn well pleases. That woman!

So all that I got to do is write in this book. I sure
am writing a lot these days. My grandfather from
Minnesota kept a diary. That's where I got the idea
from. My father has the diary now. He says it was
written in ink on little notebook paper and it is held
together with string. I wonder if Penny ever wrote
anything like this when this was her room. I sure
would like to read something that she wrote. All I
have to go by is what people tell me about her. That
she was pretty. That she was fun. Nana says that she
was spoiled rotten. Sometimes Nana says to me,
"You're worse than your damn mother."

I have pictures of her. My mother was a beautiful
woman. She was always smiling. And she was tall.
Almost five feet eight inches tall. My father told me
that with her hair and her heels, she was over six
feet tall. I think he was joking because he didn't like
her being taller than him.

Last summer when he was here I asked him if
there was anything that made Penny mad, really
mad, besides Nana. He said, "White girls." Nothing
got Penny's blood boiling like white girls. He said that
she said that when she was going to Boyle Heights
High School the white girls hated the black girls but
not the Hispanic girls, so the black girls hated the
white girls but not the Hispanic girls. He said Penny
said that if a white boy ever got caught dating a
black girl that the white girls in school would stop
talking to him. Then my father would joke to Penny,
"Thank God I never went to that high school." And
Penny would burst out laughing.

Wait a minute I have to come up for air.

OK. I'm back now. But the batteries are getting low.

Looking at her pictures it's hard to imagine Penny mad and fighting with Nana. But I know that it's true or Penny wouldn't have moved out. I wonder if Penny ever saw the things that I saw. What bothers me the most about Nana is that she's a liar. She lied to my father when she said I could come see him this summer. She lied to me when she said I could go. But most of all are the lies she tells to Grandpa. Actually they are secrets and lies. But every day is a lie.

Nana always tells us, "Don't you dare say anything to anybody. Because if you do Grandpa and I would get divorced. We'd lose our house and everything. You two would have to go live in foster homes. I'm the only one that wants you two, ya know."

So me and Raymond have never said anything even though we know that what she does is wrong. She is living a big lie.

Batteries are running out. Gotta go!

It Is Wednesday
May 6, 1992
Still grounded

Remember Marvin Sigger from my school who got shot looting a Korean store and was in a coma? He died.

We studied geography in school today. When the teacher asked what's the capital of Minnesota, almost by instinct my hand shot up in the air. I told her, "The capital of Minnesota is St. Paul, just west of Lake Elmo."

9

From the Diary of P.A. Thayer

Friday Jan 28 1955   *day 28*
33° below zero at sun up. Wow!

Pay Day. And the day in which I did nothing at work. I did go see the Swift doctor. Guess I've got a rupture and also something wrong with the old ticker. Lite work you know. Going to work with Kate tonite.

Jan 29 Sat 1955   *day 29*

A lot warmer this A.M. Don't know the exact temp.
Kate called Aunt Verna last nite and told her all our trouble. She will be here as soon as she can arrange it. I have to call her today and tell her something else that she should know.

Well I called her and told her. She will be here Sun eve
sometime. She will stay at her daughter Janice Sun nite
and I will go get her Monday morn.

~

Jan 30 Sun 1955   *day* 30

I went out last nite with Freddie. Girl next door. Under
handi cap. Ma, Pa, and Ken were along. We went to the
Paper Union dance. I came to one conclusion with two
tails on it. Freddie is either very dum or profoundly smart.

Well it is evening now. Kate has gone to work at Idle
Hour. Larry & Chris are asleep. Steve and Jim are not.

Things between Kate and I look pretty hopeless. The
longer this thing goes on the more confused I get. I think
there are things that Kate has not told me. I just don't
understand what is going on inside her. The way it looks
to me is that she still loves me, and loves Les very little. I
really do not know.

She plans on leaving after Larry's birthday which is not
too far away. In the mean time I must find a way to care
for the Boys. (Verna? Freddie? Fern? Welfare?) I don't
know where to turn.

Kate suggested that I leave and she stay with the kids.
Well as I see it that would not be a solution to our
problem. Would merely multiply it (my opinion).

I would like to see Kate have the kids but I don't think
that is what she wants.

The way I figure it. It will cost me about $250 per Mo
in payments and care for the children. In January I made
around $350. Can I make it or not? I think I can.

Perhaps I'll call in for vacation tomorrow. Would give
me more time to dope some of this out. I've sure got to go
into high gear as time of Kate's departure is less than
3 weeks off. So far only 5 people in the whole world know
about this mess but it looks as tho more must know sooner
or later.

O heck guess I'll fill the stove and go to bed. Verna
hasn't called yet. It's 10:55. Wonder if she got into town or
not.

Stinking business!

⌒

Jan 31 Monday 1955   *day* 31

+14°. Very nice day today. Warm sunshine and all.

Well Verna was here today she gave us some good
advice. I think Kate and I will go to the welfare dept and
see what they can do for us in the way of care for the kids.

I've got the painful duty of telling Freddie not to spend
too much time here. And yet I don't wish to hurt her in
any way. I think she is my best friend. At least I can cry on
her shoulder. So I hope I can be truthful about the whole
thing. It is my belief that she could take care of my boys
as well as any one.

But for those who think immoral thoughts and have evil
tongues, I must keep those things from scarring my sons if
I possibly can. I think I (we) can work something out some
way.

I told mom about it. She and Verna are of the same
mind. So with two people of wisdom such as these and

with Freddie who is young and vital on my side, how can I possibly go wrong. Thank God for them all.

I can't help but wonder if this ordeal is not meant to prepare me for things to come. I can feel a change in myself already. I hope it is for the best.

I have another problem which looks like it may be somewhat troublesome. Keeping Mrs. Walker out of my life and my boys life. I don't want that kind of help. I now believe I can handle things and would like to try it for myself.

I hope I am tactful enough to handle it without hurting any one.

Kate just went down town after her pay. Said she would be back a little after 9:00. Hope so.

Boy I sure am writing a lot these days. Makes me feel good. Maybe some day I can read it all and laugh. Or at least not feel like crying any way.

I only hope that the Lord will smile on Kate and be with her always so that she will have smooth sailing from now on. Oh Heavenly Father Bless her for her childrens sake and her own. Amen.

10

Steve—Letter to Angela

January 19, 1992
Just past midnight

Lake Elmo, Minnesota
Full Moon

Dear Angela,

A little warmer here. In fact, today was the first day in almost a month the temperature climbed above freezing. Tomorrow is Martin Luther King Jr.'s birthday, but I have to work. Newsrooms never close.

I've got a bird feeder outside my bay window. I get more squirrels than birds, but almost every day a Mr. and Mrs. Cardinal stop by for lunch. I walk right up to the glass and watch them. They don't mind me at all. You should see how red Mr. Cardinal looks in the wintertime when he is surrounded by all of the white snow.

Those first days home from the hospital after you were born were pretty hectic. I was still making a living parking cars. My dreams of being a movie star had all but evaporated.

Now Penny was out of work and we had a baby to support. When we learned Penny was pregnant we managed to scrape together five thousand dollars for a down payment on a house in Van Nuys. It was just a small house, but it was our dream house. After two years of apartment living we felt like we were in heaven.

We brought you home from the hospital and put you in your crib. Your mother climbed into bed, and I'm afraid that's where she stayed.

Penny just wasn't bouncing back. She'd always been a sleepyhead, so at first we wrote it off to her having her first child. But as the weeks dragged by she actually seemed to be getting worse. She was bedridden most of the time. She slept a lot. I took care of you. Well, I took care of you as best as I could. You were a pretty good baby. I enjoyed making you smile. I hated changing your diapers . . . you little poophead! Nana would come over and help out. She was always wanting to take you home with her until Penny was feeling better, but Penny wouldn't hear of it. Even when those two talked nice to each other, they were still fighting.

In the beginning doctors weren't much help. They just said fatigue was natural after childbirth. The thing of it was, your mother had always been so full of life. She was the easiest person in the world to make laugh. Her favorite show was *Saturday Night Live*. Anytime John Belushi showed his face she started laughing. Couldn't stop. She had a newborn baby, she had a new house, it should have been the happiest time of her life. But she was growing sadder every day. I thought it might be some kind of new-mother-depression-syndrome, like you see on Oprah. But finally Penny said, "There's something wrong with me." So we switched doctors and we switched hospitals and Penny underwent some tests.

It was a day I'll never forget. It was raining, that slow dispiriting rain you have in Los Angeles. No thunder. No lightning. Just rain. Penny was lying in the hospital bed and I was sitting beside her. We were waiting for the doctor. Neither one of us were talking. We were just staring out the window at the lousy weather. We both knew there was something wrong. We just hoped it wasn't too serious. After awhile the doctor came into the room. He was from India. Had a very heavy accent. But he was nice. Very professional. Penny really liked him. He held Penny's hand while he talked. It took him a minute to get around to it, but he finally told us that it was sickle-cell anemia. He told us about the different treatments available, but it was just talk. We knew there was no cure. The only thing I remember Penny saying that day was, "I don't want to die in the hospital. Take me home, Steven."

Well, Angel, it's after 1 A.M. now. On the nights I write to you, I don't get any other writing done. The only new vocabulary word I came up with is *syndrome*. Look it up, memorize it, and then send me the definition. OK?

I love you, Angel. See you in the summer.

Steve

11

Angela's Diary

It Is Thursday
May 7, 1992
It is VE Day

VE Day is the day World War II ended in Europe
with victory! My father taught me that last summer.
It's important because my grandfather from
Minnesota fought in that war, but in the Pacific
Ocean.

It was raining on the night that Raymond's father
killed himself. My father told me that story one day
last summer too. He said Penny told it to him often.
Grandpa doesn't like to talk about my uncle James.
Even Nana gets sad when his name comes up. James
was Penny's older brother. My father said Penny
loved James very much. And James loved her. Not
like me and Raymond fighting all the time. Maybe

they fought when they were little but by the time
James died they were almost grown up.

Raymond had just been born. He was living in our
house on the hill and so was James. But Raymond's
mother was nowhere to be found. Probably because
she was on drugs.

Everybody says that James was the nicest person
in the world. But that he was moody. Dark quiet
moods is what everybody says about him.

It was in the springtime and it had been raining
for a week. One night Miss Crist across the street
called our house and said there was a man sitting on
the roof next door. She had called the police and she
was alerting all of the neighbors. Nana and Grandpa
and Penny ran outside to see for themselves. Sure
enough there was my uncle James sitting on the roof
of the house next door. In the rain. The people who
lived in the house back then were very upset. They
wanted James off of their roof. Grandpa was trying
to coax him down while Nana was yelling up at him.
But James was just sitting up on the roof like he
wasn't listening to anybody. When the police got
there they said that James would have to come down
or he would go to jail. But James would not come
down for the police either. Finally the police called
the fire department. The firemen put a ladder up to
the house. Then a policeman went up the ladder and
brought James down. They didn't hurt him or
anything. Just put handcuffs on him. James was in
one of his silent moods.

Grandpa begged the police not to take him to jail
since he didn't hurt nobody. That he was just upset

about his girlfriend and he had a new baby. But the
police said that because he was on somebody else's
property and because they had to go to the trouble of
calling a fire truck that James would have to spend
the night in jail.

Nana ordered Penny to go in the house. Penny ran
into the house and upstairs to her room. She went
over to the window and watched as they put James
into the back of the police car. Penny could see her
brother's face pressed against the police car window,
which was speckled with raindrops. She thinks he
looked up at her with a sad smile as the police car
pulled away. She remembered it so well because it
was the last time that she ever saw James alive.

It was almost 5 o'clock in the morning and there
was a pounding at the front door. Penny woke up.
She went to her window. It was still dark. It was still
raining. The pounding on the door continued. Penny
said she was not quite awake, but standing on the
sidewalk in front of the house was her brother,
James. He smiled up at her.

Penny went to the top of the stairs. Grandpa
opened the front door. Nana was standing behind him
in her nightgown. At the door were two deputies
from the sheriff's department. They told Grandpa
that James was dead. Nana started wailing. Grandpa
held her in his arms.

Penny ran back to her room and over to the
window. She looked down at the sidewalk but James
was gone. She ran back to the top of the stairs.

The deputies said that James had hung himself

with his shirt in his jail cell. He had been dead for a couple of hours. He was nineteen years old.

Penny told my father that even years later she was sure that she had seen James standing on the sidewalk that rainy morning. She said that she couldn't explain it, but that she was sure it was James. I think so too. I think my uncle James loved his little sister so much that he just stopped by on his way to heaven to say goodbye. It was not too long after that night that Penny left home.

I like to think that they're together now. My mother Penny and my uncle James.

12

From the Diary
of P.A. Thayer

Feb 1 1955 Tuesday   *day* 32
+19°

   The past is dead. The future is alive. I must look at it
like this in order to survive. In order to live.
   4:45 P.M. I called in for my vacation and got it. Went to
Doctor Wolke today. Got to go back Thurs for a complete
check up. Kate went down town to get things for Ruth's
shower which is Friday.
   Freddie was here up till five minutes ago. She took
Steve and went over to Walkers. Said she will be back if
Kate don't get home soon???
   4:50 P.M. Kate just called. She'll be home in bout
20 min. (We'll see.) Says she has to work tonite at Idle
Hour. Must be there at 6:00. Here I am tied down again.
Course the $ will come in handy . . . but darn it anyhow.
Back to the wall any way you look at it. Wanted to go

treasure hunting for the winter carnival medallion tonite, same as I wanted to last nite, and I guess the same as it has been for the last 6 years. Stuck. Got to get out of rut as soon as possible in order to maintain sanity.

Kate told me she is leaving me Feb 19. Where did I fall down? What have I done wrong? Where will this all lead? Why? Getting all choked up again! Ticker acting up again! It is getting almost too much to bear.

Kate has 16 minutes to get here as it is near 6 o'clock.

Wish it was summertime. Perhaps I'd go fishing or something like that, or go for a walk in the woods all alone so I could think this thing out and talk with the Lord where there is peace and quiet.

7 P.M. Well Kate was here. We had a little supper and then I took her to work. Fern watched the kids. Kate was pretty well lit when she came home. Les brought her to the front steps then took off like a bird. I don't think he can face me. I intend to make him do just that soon tho. He won't get out of this without some trouble.

One more hr and the big boys go to bed. 2 more hrs and Steve goes to bed. As for Jim I hope he is asleep for the nite already.

8:30. Everyone asleep but Steve and me and I think Steve is about to go to bed. As for me . . . who knows?

The nights and days are all the same. Pace the floor by day and sleep at nite so I can pace the floor in the day time. May as well turn them around. Neither has any meaning. Some day I hope things will be better.

To any one who should read this nonsense my advice is to lay this down and go out and make a friend. Do it now before it is too late. Some one on whose shoulder you can cry when cry you must. Some one who will hold your hand and say I'll help you in any way I can. Those very words will put you back on the road to recovery. So put this down and find a new friend, or refind an old one.

Writing this way is like talking to ones self. There is not much meaning to it but it does get your troubles out where you can see them somewhat more clearly. And they do seem less important and less serious when you see them written down. I hope no one will ever read this that will be hurt by the contents or implications that I have recorded on these pages, for they are for my eyes alone and meant to clear my mind. Most of these words are just passing thoughts, and not wishing all of my thoughts to pass into oblivion, I will write some of them down.

This has been a long day for me. Kate has been gone almost all day. The boys have been reasonably good today. Altho my temper has been very bad. I am very tired but I do not want to go to bed. I keep wishing and hoping that someone would drop in and pound some sense into me, or just come in and talk and kind of get my mind off all this mess that I am in.

So there you are and here I am. Still with my back to the wall and still fighting.

13

Steve—Letter to Angela

Feb 2, 1992   Lake Elmo, Minnesota
Sunday night   Groundhog's Day

Dear Angela,

The groundhog saw his shadow today so that means six more weeks of winter, or basketball, or something like that.

This is the story of the Flying Christmas Tree. The memory of it is so vivid because this fully decorated, fully illuminated blue spruce was thrown at me.

My parents never had much money. But there was always food in the house. Lots of it. And when we woke up on Christmas morning there were toys under the tree. Lots of toys. Looking back on it now, I wonder how they ever afforded them.

Christmas Eve was always spent at my father's house in South St. Paul. He remarried, you know. Raised another family ... though his first son from that marriage died of leukemia. When I think of Christmas Eve I think of us driving down Highway 61 to my father's house. Years after his death, I was still driving down Highway 61 to spend Christmas Eve with my stepmother and my second family. Those are my most treasured memories of Christmas.

However, Christmastime with Kate and Les was another story. Like I said, Christmas Day was nice enough, toys and all. It was those weeks leading up to Christmas that turned your grandmother Kate and your grandpa Les into lunatics.

One year, late at night, we heard our parents fighting down in the basement. We just pulled the pillows over our heads and went back to sleep. No big deal. Back in those days we burned our trash in an incinerator in the basement . . . I hated it . . . filled the whole house with smoke. The day after the fight I was down in the basement burning the trash when I noticed wrapped Christmas presents stacked behind the incinerator. At first I believed Kate and Les were trying to hide them from us kids. Cute, I thought. But as I riffled through the presents I noticed that a couple of them were burned . . . like somebody had tried to stuff them into the incinerator.

My mother was born Esther Katherine Walker. But she so hated the name *Esther* that all her life she was called *Kate*. When she got married she had *Katherine* legally made her first name. But the thing of it is, Angel, us kids didn't know that. We grew up believing her name was Katherine. One day while we were going through her cedar chest with her . . . she kept her life in this big cedar chest and she loved showing it to us—wedding dress, family photos, that kind of stuff . . . anyway, one night we came across an old legal document that read, Esther Katherine Walker. Needless to say, this sent Esther Katherine's children into hysterics.

When you're a kid, or worse, a teenager, and you find out that your mother's name is Esther, the laughter can be uncontrollable. Believe me, we didn't laugh long. She got mad as hell and the name *Esther* was never mentioned again.

A couple of years later, we were putting the finishing touches on the Christmas tree. It was late. My mother had had a few beers. She insisted on hanging the tinsel herself. We were never allowed to help with this part of the decorating. This might have been how the argument started, I don't remember. I do remember that the tree was where it was every year, in the big bay window in the dining room. I was standing in the doorway between the dining room and the living room trading smart-ass remarks with my mother, who was itching for a fight with every sip of her beer. I can't recall what it was she finally said to me that pissed me off, but I distinctly remember my reply:

"Yeah, whatever you say . . . Esther!"

Big mistake.

Esther Katherine Walker grabbed the tree with both hands, lifted it off the floor, and threw it at me. The tree went flying through the dining room like a missile, just missing my head. Since the tree was still plugged in, the red and blue lights sailed by my nose in full illumination. The little angel on top of the tree went flying by sideways. Then the electric cord reached its end and was yanked from the socket, sparks flying everywhere. The tree finally came to a landing in the living room, scaring the hell out of the dog.

I don't know what happened next, or why any of it happened at all. I just remember that Christmas tree flying through the room. I would have thought it was physically impossible. But if you have a hot temper, a few drinks in you, and a smart-ass teenager in the house, I guess extraordinary strength is possible. Funny how the things back then that were so traumatic, often pathetic. I can't help but look back at now and laugh.

I loved my mother, Angel. I probably should have said it to her while she was alive.

OK, for your next letter I want you to tell me the definition of *vivid* and *extraordinary*. I love you, Angel. See you this summer.

Steve

14

Angela's Diary

It Is Friday
May 8, 1992
Just another night in my room

My father says it is important to leave a written
record so that your children and your grandchildren
will know how you lived. The way I feel these days I
don't think I'll be around to have children, but I'd
still like to write about my grandpa because even
though he didn't become a champion, he was still a
great boxer. Almost famous.

His last fight was against Kid Can at the old
auditorium in 1955. If he had won that fight that
night he says he would have fought a contender in
the Garden. When I was a little girl and I heard
people say that, I used to picture my grandpa fighting
with a container in the garden in the backyard. Of

course they meant Madison Square Garden in New
York City. But Grandpa lost that fight and he lost half
of his sight.

The bad guy was a big Irishman named Kincaid,
but all of the fighters called him Kid Can. The black
fighters called him Tin Can Man because they
thought he was a dirty fighter. Mean as a bulldog. On
the night of the fight the big Irishman showed up at
the auditorium with a black girl on his arm.

"She was a wild and sassy thing," Grandpa told us.
"Thought she was hot stuff because she was at the
fights with a white man."

"And it was Nana?"

"Yeah, it was your Nana, all right."

You got to remember that my grandpa was not a
grandpa back then. He was a young man. He hadn't
even met Nana yet. Saw her that night for the very
first time. Grandpa was big and strong. A strapping
fellow. Said he was going to be the next Joe Louis.
But first he had to knock out Kid Can.

Kid Can fought in World War II. Grandpa was too
young for that war. But by 1955 Kid Can was getting
old and everybody thought that Grandpa could beat
him. The fight took place at way past midnight and
off the books. Raymond says that means it ain't
legal. No round limit. No TKO. Last man standing.
One thousand dollars. Winner take all. And a free
ride to the Garden.

Grandpa said the old auditorium was packed that
night. Hot and smoky. It smelled like a stinky old
tennis shoe in there, is what Grandpa told us. It was
hard to breathe. The smoke was so thick that the

people in the seats looked like ten thousand ghosts.
And the noise, it was deafening. A lot of money was
riding on the fight.

Grandpa's face was smeared with Vaseline. His
rubber mouthpiece tasted like a car tire. He was
wearing his best white shorts with a gold belt. Said
he was looking good. Nana was sitting ringside. She
caught his eye just before the bell.

"Probably the last pretty thing I ever saw out of
that eye."

After the first round Kid Can wasn't feeling so
sure of himself. But Grandpa was. And always
between the rounds Grandpa said he caught Nana
giving him the eye. Said she was distracting him.

"Shoot . . . that damn woman was flirting with the
both of us."

According to Grandpa it was a real free-for-all that
night. There were low blows and sucker punches,
kicking and swearing and name calling. A real
slugfest and then some. By the end of the fifth
round, Grandpa had big welts on his face.

For most of the fight Grandpa thought he had the
best of it, but near the end of the tenth round
Grandpa crossed his feet and slipped. Kid Can caught
him with a right hook and Grandpa went down. He
never really recovered. But he still lasted two more
rounds.

It was in the twelfth. Grandpa was trying to catch
his breath up against the ropes when Kid Can
started wailing on him. Jabbing at him. Grandpa was
bleeding from his nose and his mouth. His corner
was yelling at him to take the count. "Go down!" they

kept yelling. But Grandpa, who was pinned against
the ropes, would not give up. Said he was going to
the Garden. Said he would die trying. That's when it
happened.

Grandpa let his arms drop to his sides. Said his
arms were like lead. So heavy he just couldn't hold
them up anymore. Kid Can was furious because
Grandpa wouldn't go down. So Kid Can put all of his
might into one last punch. Grandpa's head was
hanging low. Said he could count the blood drops on
the tops of his shoes. Then he saw Kid Can's right
uppercut. And there was nothing he could do but
take it.

"Kid's fist went into my eye like a knife."

The uppercut caught his left eye and sent Grandpa
spinning through the ropes and onto the cement floor
of the old auditorium. Grandpa said the floor was all
wet and sticky but it might have been from his blood.
He wasn't out cold because he could hear the referee
counting to ten. And he could hear the crowd roaring
like a pack of hungry lions.

"Funny thing is, while I was laying there bleeding
to death all I kept thinking about was your Nana . . .
that wild and sassy woman that came to the fight
with the Kid."

Then he was out cold.

When he woke up he was in the county hospital.
The doctors told him he might never be able to see
out of his left eye again. And he never has.

"So you stole his girlfriend, didn't you, Grandpa?"

"That's right. I stole the Kid's girlfriend."

Grandpa never boxed again. But he worked hard

and saved enough money to open his own gym. And
to marry Nana and raise a family. Two families. First
Penny and James. And now me and my cousin,
Raymond.

It was last year sometime. I was at the gym with
Grandpa and Raymond watching the fighters. This big
old crusty white man wandered in. He smelled. I
think he lived on the street. After awhile he shuffled
over to Grandpa. At first I thought he was just a
beggar. But then Grandpa shook his hand and said,
"Hey, Kid, how you doing?"

He mumbled something back and then Grandpa
gave him two dollars and told him to go get himself
some coffee. The crusty man grunted and shuffled
away, looking back over his shoulder at the fighters
in the ring.

On the way home that night Grandpa told us the
story. Told us that was Kid Can, the man who
punched his eye out. The man who made him half-
blind way back in 1955.

"Did he get to fight in the Garden?" Raymond
asked.

"No," Grandpa said, "he never got to go to the
Garden. That was just something they told us to get
us in the ring."

"He probably never got the money either, did he,
Grandpa?"

"No, probably not."

15

From the Diary
of P.A. Thayer

Feb 3 Thurs 1955   *day 34*

Another beautiful day. Went again to Dr. office. Got a check up. The Doc said he was pleased. Gave me enough pills for a month for $1.25.

Went to the welfare today. They sent me to family services. Got an appointment for tomorrow.

Kate is working at the Idle Hour tonite. Then she is going to look for the treasure after work up around the capitol some where. Hope she finds it.

I wish this business would clear itself up. It's getting me down. It's getting hard on Kate too and she has an awful lot ahead of her. And I still love her. I don't want to see her hurt no matter what.

Hope I can find a good home for the boys. I'm afraid we're going to lose Jimmy and perhaps Steve too. I'm going to try or I should say fight to keep them as long as I can one way or another.

Well I'm alone again tonite. Wish I had someone to talk to. But I must come to realize that I will have a lot of lonely nites from now on. I really don't intend to stay single if I can help it.

***

Feb 4 Friday 1955   *day 35*

Down rite nasty day. Snow lots of snow. Very rough.

Got the chains from Uncle Al today and put them on the car. Hope they help.

I was at family services today. They will do what they can to help.

Well Eddie Meyer got layed off today. So he went home to Wisconsin. Said he was going fishing.

***

Feb 5 Sat 1955   *day 36*

Well its 10:10 P.M. Kate is sorting out her stuff getting ready to leave me. Hope family services can find a good person to care for the kids.

Been thinking a lot about big brother. Should write Reggie a letter one of these days and let him in on the dope.

I still can't believe that Kate is leaving me. Wish I could figure it out. I don't see how it could be Les. It don't seem possible. Don't know what I'm going to do. I hope when it actually happens it will be clean so no one gets hurt.

Must watch myself very closely at all cost to keep the boys name clean. It will be hard on them as it is.

⌒

Feb 6 Sunday 1955   *day 37*

Well it is now 6:05 A.M. Kate isn't home yet. Maybe this is it. I don't know. I've been awake since 2:45 A.M. awaiting her arrival. Can't help but wonder if something isn't wrong. I wish she would either phone or come home or something. I hate to call the police about this.

Kate got home at 6:20. Everything OK.

Well my vacation is over. Got to go back to work tomorrow. Larry and Chris are up. The peace is shattered for the day. 12 hrs of bedlam and mayhem. Everything from soup to nuts. Mostly nuts.

8:15 P.M. Good old faithful Zeke. Sitting with the kids again. Everybody goes out but me, and here I sit, sit sit! Even have to patch my own O'alls. Change diapers, fill bottles, wash dishes, and me with a wife. Kate goes to work for 4 hrs and spends 4 hrs with her boyfriend, while faithful old Zeke does her work for her at home!!!

10:30. Well I've cooled off a little now.

Guess I'll go to bed.

⌒

Feb 7 Monday 1955 *day* 38

9:35 P.M. Kate filed federal income tax today. We get $132 back. She was only down town about 6 hrs. She brought Les home with her. So Freddie says, which makes me kind of sore. Don't know if its right or not but I think someone is going to wind up in the garbage can head first. And it isn't going to be me.

Boy I sure wish this was all over and done with. Kids are all asleep and here I am alone again. Its very hard. Here I go feeling sorry for myself again and that's no good.

Think I'll read the paper a little and go to bed.

⌒

Feb 8 Tues 1955 *day* 39

It is now about 8:30 P.M. +9° degrees. Snowed a little.

At present the future is very dim and unreal to me. I wonder just what runs through Kate's head when she thinks of leaving the family, our home, and all we've worked for these years. I don't understand it. She says she don't love me any more. She says she loves Les. Does she? I find it hard to believe. I visualize Kates future as much unhappiness and sadness.

And in the meantime Zekie old boy you have got to look out for your own hide. When you get all squared away maybe you can get a crack at this happiness stuff.

That week I spent on lite work and my vacation week

constitutes the longest time I've been out of the freezer in
over 6 years. And I think it did me a lot of good. Both in
body and mind.

It gives me a lot of pleasure to put down my thoughts
on paper. It seems to give them some meaning. Thoughts
are funny things, if you don't stop them they will flit by
with out any meaning what so ever.

Well enough B.S. for this eve. Think I'll go to bed.

~

Feb 9 Wed 1955   *day 40*

7:45 A.M. +25°. Warm huh?

2:00 P.M. Boy do I feel sick! Stayed home today. Called
in sick slept till near noon.

I just called Family Services.

A Mrs. Goldberg said she would get in touch with us
soon. Hope so.

Well Kate went to work at 5:00. She had supper ready
when she left so I fed the kids and washed the dishes. And
so now here I sit. It's not even 6:00 yet. One of these days
I'm going to cut loose and really have me a time.

It is hard for a man to start a new faze of his life in a
hole. One which will take him years to dig out of. When I
met Kate I had nothing, but I had no debts or children
either. Now as she is about to leave me I have nothing,
plus debts and four children. Will I ever have the nerve to
remarry and face the chance of the same mistakes again?
Kate walks away with just what she came with . . . nothing!
Free as a bird. No debts, no kids, no nothing. Just herself

and her conscience. Altho I do not envy her in her choice
of future mates.

O! Well. I still love her tho. We have less than ten days
left together as she is leaving on Feb 19. What can be
done in less than ten days? I will not stop trying however.
It is hard when I have so little time each day with her.
Enough of the dismal things. Feeling sorry for my self?
You bet I am. I'm very frankly bored stiff with the whole
mess.

Think I'll close this book for today. I wrote too much
already.

16

Steve—Letter to Angela

Feb 21, 1992   Lake Elmo, Minnesota
Friday night   Cold, but bearable

Dear Angela,

These days are the dead of winter. The fun of snow is behind us, and spring is still a month away. It's a good thing I have a pretty girl to write to on nights like this.

As I've said before, I loved my stepfather, but I never liked him. He kept telling us that a good Depression would do us kids some good. It didn't appear to do him much good. The Depression, followed by World War II, just seemed to make him a mean old man. He came from a generation, or maybe it was just a family, where children were supposed to be seen and not heard. Believe me, that wasn't us. Not only were we four boys his stepchildren, but we were also independent and mouthy little things. Brats! But he never stopped trying to mold us. The belt was his weapon of choice. I lost count of how many times he beat my butt with that belt for something I did wrong. My skin would be red for days. The message he wanted to deliver was . . . don't ever do it again. But the message I got was . . . do it again out of spite, but next time don't get caught. And that's exactly what I did. I was bad!

Les was a big, gruff man with a loud voice and a personality to match. Over and over I asked myself how my mother could divorce my father, the nicest man in the world, and marry this . . . this . . . other guy. She wasn't even drinking back then.

The old man was always saying stuff like, "I'll knock your head clear off your shoulders, mister." Or, "You'll be chasing your head up Earl Street, bub." His most memorable line was the one he used while fighting with my mother: "You no good lousy bitch!" Even today if I want to make fun of one of your uncles I'll say to him, "You no good lousy bitch!" I shouldn't be writing you this stuff, but it's a family joke.

There were seven of us living in that big house on Wilson Avenue, but there was only one bathroom. The old place had one of those ancient toilets where the tank hung on the wall just below the ceiling. Then to flush it we had to pull on this long chain that hung down from the tank. With seven people fighting to pee and poop, the toilet spilled over its banks more often than the Mississippi River. One day the old man says he's going to fix that toilet for good.

"Everybody stay out of the bathroom until I'm done."

So the old man grabs his hammers and wrenches and heads off down to the basement, where he disconnects the drainpipe. I don't know which one of us four boys didn't hear the order, but one of us walked into the bathroom, took a whiz, and then pulled the chain. Between the gushing water and the old man screaming down in the basement, I thought it was an earthquake. The whole house was shaking. As soon as I realized that somebody had emptied the toilet onto the old man's head, I tore out of the house. Within seconds I was running down Wilson laughing like a hyena. And my three brothers were right behind me. I don't remember which one of us actually flushed the toilet on him, but I like to think it was me.

He was forever trying to put grease in our hair, especially on Sunday mornings when we'd dress for church.

"Let's get some grease in that hair, boy."

We wanted to look like John Kennedy or the Beatles. The old man wanted us to look like Herbert Hoover. He'd smear this god-awful stuff called Brylcream into those callused, yellow hands of his and he'd rub it into our hair. A little dab was supposed to do ya, but he'd rub a big gob into our heads until it hurt.

The worst things were his haircuts. He had this electric shears that sounded like a buzz saw, and that's the way he used it. We'd have to climb up on this stool in the kitchen and sit there while the old man buzzed our heads with those shears, just like we were sheep. He'd cut until we were crying, and nearly bald. "Ah, stop your blubbering." Then he'd yell, "Next!" To this day I wear my hair long just to spite the old man . . . and I don't care how many years he's been dead.

But you know, Angel, I think in the end the old S.O.B.

was proud of us, the way we turned out and all. He certainly left his mark on us. And not just on our butts, either.

Look up *Depression* for me, with a capital *D*.

I love you. See you this summer.

Steve

17

Angela's Diary

It Is Saturday
May 9, 1992

When I was only seven years old I almost didn't get any birthday cake on my birthday. We only get birthday cake twice a year. On my birthday and on Raymond's birthday. Because it was my birthday I was being extra good all day long. Then just before supper Raymond started a fight while we were watching <u>Happy Days</u> on TV.

"You think you're white like those people, don't you, cracker?"

That started a big fight and Nana came running in from the kitchen. The TV was turned off and we had to sit in chairs with our mouths shut. And no cake. I started crying.

"You mean I don't get any birthday cake?"

"I told you about fighting. I'm sick of it!"

Then Raymond opened his big mouth. "What's so special about your birthday? Your mother died because you were born."

That ain't true, but I believed it for a long time because Nana didn't even say anything. I was only seven. Sickle-cell anemia is a disease that is inherited. It is most common in people whose ancestors came from Africa. Penny was born with sickle-cell. I didn't give it to her. Doctors checked me when I was a baby and I did not inherit sickle-cell. Two years ago my father took me to the doctors for a checkup and he made them check again just to be sure. I do not have it.

So anyway I got sent to my room with no supper that night and I cried myself to sleep. I can't remember if I was crying most because I didn't get any birthday cake or because I thought I made my mother die.

I woke up when Grandpa got home from the gym. It was late, but it was before midnight so it was still my birthday. Everyone was in bed. I tiptoed down the stairs and peeked into the kitchen. Grandpa was cutting himself a big piece of cake. At first I didn't think he saw me standing in the doorway. But then he cut a second piece.

"C'mon, Stubby, let's you and me have some cake."

So I sat at the kitchen table with Grandpa and I had the biggest piece of birthday cake I ever had in my life. And while we were eating our cake Grandpa

told me stories about Penny. How when she was a
kid she had the biggest sweet tooth he had ever
seen. He said when she was a little girl he called her
Chocolate Face, and it didn't have anything to do
with the color of her skin.

18

From the Diary of P.A. Thayer

February 11 Friday 1955   *day 42*

9:15 P.M. −2°. A bit warmer altho the prediction is for −20° for the lo tonite. Nice huh?

Henry started this eve. The first time I tried since Wed nite. Gas line must have thawed.

Today was a long day for me at work. I'm kind of tired. I've got to go to the Doc tomorrow morn. Also get that tire fixed. I've got to go to family services Monday morn at 8:30 and see a Mr. Lee??? Suspense is a rough thing.

Well my coffee is done so I think I'll have some and read a little and go to bed.

Feb 12 Saturday 1955   *day 43*

7:45 P.M. Well Kate has gone to work and I am awaiting Fern so I can go out. I'm just about to put the big boys to bed. I'll leave Steve for Fern to stow away. I sure hope she makes it on time as I don't wish to be late.

I was to the Doctor this morn. I'm getting better it seems. I go back when my pills are gone. I feel much better than I did when I was last there.

Every one seems to have an idea of what is going on here but no one knows for sure. If they did the fur would sure fly. I hope they don't find out till the time comes. At which time I will be wearing my suit of armor.

All for now.

~

Feb 13 Sunday 1955   *day 44*

Had a nice time last nite. Took Freddie to Alarys. And I really believe she was just a little bit shocked at the floor show (Strip Tease).

Melody of Love they say was first published in 1910. Wayne King has a nice version of the song where the melody is but background music for a nice spoken recitation. I'll try to get the record.

The grand exit (explosion) is set for Saturday next. After that who knows? I don't. I don't even pretend to.

Was up to the folks for awhile this afternoon. Darn near went to sleep on the floor while I was there.

Kate has gone to work again at the Idle Hour, and again I am left alone with the boys. The job isn't so bad it's just

the hours that get me. When everyone is out a visitin etc.
I must sit at home and play nursemaid to a bunch of
Indians.

O well such is life I guess. Who knows what tomorrow
will bring? Perhaps something real nice will crop up.

⌒

Feb 14 Monday 1955   *day 45*

10:55 P.M. Guess I didn't accomplish anything. Family
Services can't take the kids. Now what do I do?

Took Kate down town to get her pay. Said she would
be home around 10. Well what happened???

O have I learned things today. Boy O Boy. Got
something for Kate for Valentine's Day. But don't think I'll
give it to her after the things I learned today.

Most of my thoughts are too dark to put on paper,
so I won't. They would be poor reading. However I'll
still take her back if she wants to come. But I will be
harder to please from now on. As I've written before I've
learned things, lots of things. Things I haven't wanted to
know and things that I wish I'd have known a long time
ago.

Poor kids. They will be the ones that this will hurt
most. Wish there was some way to spare them. But I don't
see how. Have I done everything possible? I don't know.
Heaven help me.

⌒

Feb 15 Tuesday 1955   *day 46*

8:30 P.M. Not much sleep last nite. Not much conversation around here. But I think her foot is out the door. Just not sure. Will know in a day or so.

We're in very bad shape $. Don't know just how I'll pull out of it. But try I must. This whole business is eating up the cash just a little at a time. Got to do some fancy scraping to come out of it.

Feb 17 Thurs 1955   *day 48*

Nice day. Larry's birthday. 5 yrs old today.

Kate saw minister this P.M. I talked to Les this P.M. May be got a foot hold. Don't know. Hope so. Love her so.

Placement for kids??? Awful hard to do.

Feb 18 Friday 1955   *day 49*

Rain and ice on streets. Nasty today.

Well Kate has gone to work. She is leaving tomorrow? (I hope not.) I'm still trying. I just finished dishes. It is now a bit after 9:00. I was down to South St. Paul this P.M. to get my check. Not much.

Les thinks that all I think of is the kids and money. But he is wrong. Dead wrong. True I spoke to him yesterday of money, a lot about it. But it was meant to impress him with the scope and importance of this thing. It's very hard

for a man to speak of Love to another man, especially if
the other man is stealing your wife. What manner of man
must he be? A thief? Maybe. A bum? Perhaps. Smooth?
Slick? Without a visible flaw? Hardly. Believe me it is a
challenge which I will not let pass. As Kate leaves this
house tomorrow, I will charge Les with her well being. All
aspects of it.

It's snowing out now. Looks like it may get deep before
it stops.

19

Steve—Letter to Angela with News Article

March 17, 1992
St. Patrick's Day

Lake Elmo, Minnesota
+50° today!

Dear Angela,

The snow is melting fast. Spring is in sight.

Did I ever tell you about our neighbor, weird Alfons Anderson? When I was growing up on Wilson Avenue he lived directly across the street from us, just like Miss Crist lives across the street from you. Is she still teaching? Anyway, Al was a Swedish man. He still spoke with that heavy Swedish accent that people here poke fun at. Me and my brothers used to play with his sons, Roland and Dana. When we were kids we all loved weird Al because he was the only adult we knew that behaved just like us . . . a big kid. He worked for a construction company and drove this dirty green truck that he parked out on Wilson day in and day out for as long as we lived there . . . and that was a long time.

We really thought he was a nice man, always helping plow the snow and start cars, and running us little boys around town. Swimming in the summer. Sledding in the winter. But apparently he behaved a lot differently around little girls. I first became suspicious of him when Roland and Dana would be called home so that they could watch *Hee Haw* with their dad. I don't know if that show is around anymore, maybe on cable somewhere, but it was a country western show written for people who married their cousins . . . and I thought the family gathering around *Hee Haw* every week was a sure sign that there was something funny going on over at the Anderson house.

One of our best friends back then was a kid named Mickey Benson. He lived up the street. He had two little sisters. I can't tell you how old the girls were, but they were pretty young because we were all kids. One day Mickey came down to our house crying his eyes out because they had to move and his parents wouldn't tell him why. But the whole family was gone within a week and we never saw Mickey again.

Anyway, the reason I'm telling you this story is that last week I picked up the *Pioneer Press* and read the enclosed article. (Read the newspaper article.)

St. Paul Man Accused of Longtime Pedophilia

A sixty-nine-year-old man whose neighbors regarded him as a genial grandfather figure for many years has pleaded guilty to molesting a three-year-old girl and is suspected by authorities of molesting neighborhood children as far back as the 1960s . . .

Then I read that it was weird Al Anderson, and they gave his Wilson Avenue address. Phones were ringing off the hook. Apparently, weird Al didn't know that the old gang from Wilson Avenue still keeps in touch. Now we know why our friend with the two little sisters suddenly moved away. I've also learned that it was those two sisters, now all grown up, who first tipped off police. They grew up never forgetting about the man who molested them when they were little. And now others girls are coming forward.

Weird Al is going to jail for three years, maybe more, and when he gets out he'll be a known sex offender. It makes me feel bad . . . kind of stupid . . . that all those years that terrible stuff was going on right across the street and we didn't even know about it. You have to understand, Angel, that child abuse was something that was not talked about back then. You kids today are much more attuned to it.

Hey, there's a good word. *Attuned.* Look it up for me. Write back.

I love you, Angel. See you in the summer.

Steve

20

Angela's Diary

It Is Sunday
May 10, 1992
Mother's Day

Another week of running home from school in less
than fifteen minutes! Go to my room! Eat supper! Go
back to my room! Go to bed! That woman!!! If I don't
get out of here this summer I'm going to cut my
wrists open! I'm going to get a gun and blow my
brains out! I'll show them!!!

OK it's later and I've cooled off a little now.

Besides, it's Mother's Day. I shouldn't be talking
like that.

Penny was seventeen years old and a senior at
Boyle Heights High School when she finally had
enough of Nana and she hit the bricks. My father
said Penny talked about those days a lot. Grandpa

told me a little about the troubled times in our house back then. And Nana still gets steaming mad whenever the subject comes up.

Grandpa says Penny grew up fast after James hung himself in that jail cell. Penny thought maybe Nana was taking her anger and sorrow out on her. Grandpa says in those days he was just too sad to get mad at anybody, even the police who took James off to jail when they really didn't have to.

It all started over boys. When Penny was seventeen she got boy-crazy. The summer before, Nana sent her up to relatives in Bakersfield for two weeks to cool off. But when Penny got back to town she was even worse.

Grandpa says Nana was just as wild when she was young. That Penny was just a kinder, gentler version. But Penny was much prettier than Nana ever was and that might have been what Nana resented. Maybe.

Penny would stay out late and then Nana would demand to know where she had been and Penny would say, "I met a rich man and we went to his mansion in Beverly Hills and we made luvvv!"

That would make Nana furious. Then Nana and Penny would get into a big fight.

"Don't you lie to me. Now where have you been?"

"Even when I tell you the truth, you think it's a lie."

"Because I know about your lies, girl."

"And I know the truth about you, woman."

Grandpa says the biggest fight was on the day he asked Penny to get along or get out. Penny and Nana

were screaming at each other right in the living
room when he got home. Nana yelled, "Go ahead, tell
him . . . tell him anything you want! Tell him just to
spite me! I dare you! I double dare you!"

"Tell me what?" Grandpa asked.

And Penny almost told him. Something. Grandpa
said he saw her lips quivering, like the words were
forming but they just wouldn't come out. Tears of
anger were in her eyes. Then Penny stormed out of
the room. Took all of her secrets with her.

Grandpa says it didn't really bother him. Didn't
think much about it. Said there are things between a
mother and a daughter that a man probably
shouldn't know. But Grandpa almost broke into tears
when he went upstairs to her room and he told
Penny that if she couldn't get along with Nana she
was going to have to leave.

"Damn shame when a man has to choose between
his wife and his daughter."

He was surprised when Penny left.

"Yup. Just packed her a suitcase, walked
downstairs, and out the front door. Never looked back
at us. Never saw so much foolish pride in a girl."

I wonder exactly what Penny knew. I wonder if
they are the same secrets me and Raymond know.
These are the things everybody says I'm too little to
understand.

Anyway Penny not only moved out of the house,
but she also dropped out of high school. I think I
know a little how she must have felt because I
remember how scared I was the day I ran away. But
I knew where I was going. To the bus station to catch

a bus to Minnesota. Penny didn't really have
anywhere to go. She sneaked in with her friend Celia
at her house, but they were a big Mexican family and
it was impossible to keep a secret.

She lived in the back of a van with a couple of
runaways for almost a year. Penny smoked pot and
tried to be a hippie but by then the hippies were like
the dinosaurs. Extinct. Once they all got stopped
by the police and they were really scared. She said
there were times when she thought of selling herself
for money. Her head really got mixed up. She always
talked about going back to school to get her GED and
then maybe her and Celia were going to go to nursing
school.

"Why did you want to be a nurse?" my father
asked her.

"So we could marry doctors, you fool."

After awhile she went back home to visit
Grandpa and to play with Raymond. And she would
even talk to Nana sometimes. But she absolutely
refused to move back home. Even though Grandpa
said she secretly wanted to. And my father also said
Penny secretly wanted to. But her pride was just too
strong.

"I'm so happy to be free I can handle anything.
Even being poor." That's what Penny said.

After bouncing around at jobs that she hated
Penny got a job in the parking garage at the big
Boneventure Hotel in downtown Los Angeles. Only
guys worked there then. She was the only girl. Penny
was the hostess with the mostess. One of the guys
was my father.

He said he enjoyed working there because the money was good and the people he got to work with were from all over the world. There were parking attendants from Ethiopia, Mexico, Thailand, Puerto Rico, France, England, and other places. He said for a white boy from the Midwest it was an experience. But of all of the people he met while parking cars he'd never met anybody like my mother.

"One day I walked through the double doors into the garage and there was this big head of hair staring me in the face . . . and you should have seen the figure it was attached to." It was Penny.

21

From the Diary
of P.A. Thayer

Feb 19 Saturday 1955   *day 50*

Well Kate left me this afternoon about 2:30. There is great sadness in my heart. Jimmy is at the Folks. The rest of the boys are still home. What must a man do to keep his wife? What must he say? Why did she leave? Will she return?

Chris says if mommie stays away too long he won't love her any more. Larry don't feel too loved he says. Steve is too young to know what has happened.

Where have I failed? What have I done that is wrong? Can I still get her back? I pray that the Lord smiles on her and also that he brings her back to me and the boys.

In a way I don't blame her. Bearing one child after another and caring for them has been no picnic.

She left most of her clothes here. Says she will come after them Wed nite. I hope the boys and I can make her

stay home and never more leave us. We all love her. I can't
bear thinking of her in a hotel room.

Well think I had best retire and see what the morrow
brings. Something good I hope.

⁓

Feb 20 Sunday 1955   *day* 51

9:15 P.M. Well I thought we had a place to put the kids
for a while. But everyone turned to their true color except
Mom. And she has no other color but the one she puts
before you. Looks like I'll have to take my vacation and
care for the kids. So there you are and here I sit.

Kate has been gone for over a day. Seems like a month.
I'm going to Family Services again tomorrow to try and
make some arrangement about the kids.

The kids are all asleep now and all is quiet about the
house.

Guess I'll go to bed.

⁓

Feb 22 Tuesday 1955   *day* 53

Last nite I went and found Kate. She don't look good.
At any rate she is coming home Sunday to take care of the
kids and I am leaving. She is coming over tomorrow to
take care of the kids while I go to the credit union to
arrange a loan to straighten out our bills.

I think while I'm out I'll see if I can't find a room close

enough to work to walk. I can save my self some money. I will have to live very close to get by.

I guess Kate went to Cumberland with Les today.

Grannie was here today. She cried a while and went home.

Such a mess stinks. Smells and has a bad odor. Thing is I still would have Kate if she would come home and be my wife. As I still love her.

I gave her . . . her ring back as I have no need for it. And perhaps she can give it to one of the boys.

Perhaps it will all come out for the best. If Les's intentions are honorable. And I hope for Kates sake they are.

~

Feb 23 Wed 1955   *day 54*

8:15 A.M. −4°. The sun is shining. Chris is up. I think Larry is awake.

Well the last week of my vacation is nearly over. No more time for my self for over a year to come. At least I will have several three-day weekends this year and that will help some. I do want to go to Chicago some time soon if I can afford it.

Steve is up. Darn it.

It's going to be a grind financially for me for the next thousand years or so. I may have to take a part time job. I've got to see how much money I need so I will know how much to borrow today. $$$$$$ Phooey!

It is now 12:15 and I am not so patiently awaiting Kate's arrival. Said she would be here at about noon. Hope she keeps her word as I have much to do. And because I want to see her just to see her.

Steve I think is taking his nap about now. I threw him at the bed anyway. Hope he sleeps.

Well it is now 5:55 P.M. Kate has been here and just left. I was to South St. Paul and arranged for a loan and rented a room in a hotel. The South St. Paul Hotel. It isn't too bad a place. Got to find a place for my car yet.

I'm going to try and send Kate $50 a month. She thinks she can get by on that. It's not much $ but we'll try it that way and see. Hope she can make it O.K. She didn't look too good when she came this noon.

I've got to go out and get me a trunk or a foot locker for my things. I'm only going to take what I need for the time being. I'll take a little more each time I come to see the kids.

I've a challenge to meet. I wonder if I can meet it? What foolish talk. Of course I can meet it. I know I can.

~

Feb 24 Thursday 1955   *day 55*

7:30 A.M. −2°. The man on the radio says it will get no warmer. It will drop all day to a low of −15° tonite. Brrr!

Ernie Ford is on TV. He's good. Lots of B.S. Steve is playing with the dish pan. Such a noise.

I imagine I had better get some of my things together to take along when I leave. That's a job I don't like. Especially when I don't want to leave in the first place. And again I say I hope it is for the best.

I'll call Family Services this afternoon and let them know just what the dope is. (Me I guess.)

Tomorrow is payday. I've got to slip down to Swift and get my check some way. Don't know just how I'll do it. Perhaps I can get Kate to watch the kids for a while.

It is now 9:00 P.M. Larry & Chris are asleep. Had Steve in bed but he is up again. So there you are.

Got to get the stove filled before I retire and turn the darn thing on full blast so we don't freeze to death in here.

~

February 26 Saturday 1955   *day 57*

10:00 A.M. Well tomorrow is the day I move out. In my opinion it is the silliest thing I've ever done. It is hard for me to believe that I will be leaving my wife. But then she has been gone a week now without much feeling toward me. So I guess it would be best if I leave when she gets here.

Earl was here. That's Les's cousin. Wanted to know just what Freddie told me Monday. Not much. He also mentioned a Joe, who ever that is. I don't like this sort of thing. Told Les about it. Boy that makes me mad to think that that guy would come out here. Where did he get my address? Wish he would keep his mess at home. I've got enough trouble of my own with out taking on some of his.

So Les is borrowing $ to keep this going huh? Well that's nice to know. I just wonder how long it would last if he should suddenly run out of that green stuff. So he hasn't got anything. Well! Well! Well! Now we are getting someplace.

Just got in touch with Kate. She says Earl has served 5 yrs in Stillwater for killing a man. Careful Zeke. Look out boy.

9:00 P.M. I've got a few of my clothes packed. Hate the job under these conditions.

Something strange. My knife is missing. My pocket knife with the yellow handle. Think the last time I seen it was Thursday when I made the what-not shelf. Darn funny that it should disappear like that. I've looked all over. I've had it for some time and would like to keep it. O. well perhaps the kids have seen it some place.

I wonder what Kate is doing tonite. Wish she were home with me where she belongs. I'm afraid Kate is in for a rough time. I don't trust Les, and Earl, who ever he is.

Saturday nite and again I sit with the kids. I wonder how many Sat nites Kate will sit with the kids. I wonder how many babysitters Les will pay for. I wonder if he really intends to marry her???

My last nite at home. Kind of a sad thing. I wish we could avoid it some way but I don't see how. I hope the kids will be O.K. This will be hard on them. Too bad they have to suffer for something over which they have no control. Makes me mad to think some bum can step in and break up a home and in the eyes of the law is blameless.

Think I'll go to bed and see if I can't get a little sleep.

22

Steve—Letter to Angela

April 5, 1992   Lake Elmo, Minnesota
Daylight Saving Time   Snow Is gone

Dear Angela,

It's raining, the first rain of spring. The grass is turning green and little buds are sprouting on the trees. I saw a robin today—in Minnesota, another sure sign of spring. It's Mother Nature getting all spruced up for your arrival in June.

The train tracks that run through Lake Elmo are about three blocks from our house. The midnight train just went by. Airplane noise drives me crazy, but there's still something romantic about the sound of a train whistle in the night. Especially on a cold, rainy night like tonight.

This is the letter I've been putting off. But summer will soon be upon us and I want you to know how things were ten years ago . . . how they really were.

With sickle-cell patients the doctors call it "crisis." But that's just a medical term for "pain." In her last weeks on this earth Penny was in a lot of pain. I only want you to know this because I want you to know how strong and courageous she was. There's nothing pretty about dying. Death is slow and ugly. Whenever I'm hurting, whenever I'm in a little bit of pain, I just think of what Penny had to go through. Then I feel downright silly.

Our insurance paid for a nurse to come to the house everyday. Penny was given painkillers, but if they worked, I couldn't tell. The nurse said if she went back to the hospital they could use intravenous drugs, probably morphine. But Penny said no to that idea. She had the kind of pain that medicine can't help.

You may be too young to understand this . . . I keep saying that, don't I? In sickle-cell patients molecules stick to one another, forming long rods inside red blood cells. These rods form in the shape of a sickle and harden. These are called blood clots. These clots are unable to squeeze through blood vessels, depriving the heart and the brain and other organs of a normal blood supply. And that's what causes so much pain. Understand all that?

While all of this was going on, you were being well taken care of at Nana's house. Nana would bring you over every day and lay you in bed next to Penny. Sometimes you and Penny would nap together. One afternoon all three of us fell asleep in the same bed . . . me, you, and Penny. When I woke up, I was afraid that you had been squished, but I found you under the blankets, and you were OK.

It was a rainy November, or maybe in my mind it just seemed to be raining all the time, but I used to sit in bed with Penny for hours at a time. I would read and write, and hold her when her pain seemed unbearable. Then we would both start crying and somehow the tears eased the pain more than the pills. We talked about you a lot. I made Penny a lot of promises. I broke most of them. I'm not proud of that. Someday soon I'm going to have to share all those broken promises with you.

Her last days were spent in and out of a coma. If Penny was in any pain then, it was impossible to tell. Sometimes I needed the nurse just to tell me if she was still alive. Finally, on the evening of November 19, 1982, just after 9 P.M. . . . Penny left us. Joined the angels in heaven.

In a way, I was relieved because Penny was free of all that pain. But then I felt guilty because maybe I was just relieved for myself that it was all over. In truth, my pain had just begun.

My own father was gone by the time Penny died. But your grandpa came over that night. He took me outside for some air. We stood in the front yard for the longest time, watching moths circle the street lamp. I don't think we even talked. I can't remember anything that was said, but it is my favorite memory of your grandpa. If ever I needed a father . . . that was the night.

I set all the clocks ahead last night. Lost an hour of sleep. Tonight I'm tired. Bedtime. Look up *intravenous* for me.

I love you, Angel. See you in just two months.

Steve

23

Angela's Diary

It Is Saturday
May 16, 1992
No smog tonight
I can see the full moon

I was just a little baby in 1982 so most of this
story I have put together from what other people
have told me. It is the story of the day my mother
was laid to rest. Everybody tells me it was the
biggest funeral they have ever seen. All of Grandpa's
fighters were there. And all of the neighbors and all
of our family and all of our friends. My father sat
right up front but Grandpa said my father was
numbed by the whole thing. Didn't say much. Kind of
glassy-eyed through the funeral. Grandpa says he
has seen that look in the eyes of fighters who don't
know what the hell hit them.

Nana brought me to the funeral and held me the whole time. She later told me, "Your daddy didn't pay you one bit of attention at your mother's funeral. It was like you was never even born. Says he's a writer . . . ha! Took that man three years to even write us a letter . . . let us know he was still alive."

The casket was open. Penny was dressed in the same white dress that she got married in on Catalina Island. Everybody who walked by said how she looked just like an angel. Last summer I asked my father to take me to Catalina Island where he and Penny got married but he said it would be too sad for him so we didn't go. Before they closed the casket they took off Penny's wedding ring and gave it to my father. I know that it cost a thousand dollars because Nana has told me a thousand times. You would think Nana paid for it. She says that ring belongs to me . . . which means it belongs to her.

Like all sad days it was raining. The funeral procession was the longest anybody had ever seen. More than a mile. We were already standing on the hillside in front of the casket and the cars were still coming through the gate. Nana was holding me tight. I shouldn't have been out there in the rain but that was part of Nana's plan. In the drizzle the Reverend Smith talked about how sad it was that Penny's days on this earth were so few. But she touched so many. She changed a lot of lives. And she left behind a beautiful little girl of her own. Me! All of the prayers were said and all of the tears were shed and then Penny was laid to rest beside her brother, James.

Nana had lost a son to suicide and now she had lost a daughter to sickle-cell anemia. She wasn't about to lose me.

Grandpa heard her say, "I ain't gonna let him take that child. What kind of father would he be? A single white man raising a little black girl out in the Valley. What kind of life would she have out there?"

At the reception at our house on the hill after the funeral Nana was going to tell my father that I was sick. That I shouldn't have been out in the rain. That I needed looking after. Too much excitement for one day and stuff like that.

Then, believe it or not, Nana was gonna kidnap me. Grandpa said she was going to leave him and Raymond behind. Her plan was to take me up to Bakersfield. She has family outside of town. Nobody knows what her plans with me were after that.

"That woman was crazy . . . she wanted you so bad," Grandpa said.

Oh yes, Nana had it all planned out. But all of her plans were for nothing. My father didn't come to the reception. A month later he sold the little house in the Valley and went back to Minnesota. Alone.

Funny how when you're a baby it's so easy to end up somewhere you don't belong. When I die I would like to be buried next to the mother that I never knew. For anybody who ever reads this please do not feel sorry for the little girl who might kill herself. I know what I am doing. My mother took her secrets to her grave, but I'm going to write them down. Because I think Penny and I saw the same things.

Nana has boyfriends. She brings them over to the

house while Grandpa is at the gym. When me and
Raymond were little they would do things right on
the couch while we were watching television. Most of
the time they would go into the bedroom, but
sometimes they did it right on the couch. Right in
front of us. This was before I knew what sex was all
about. Me and Raymond would be watching cartoons
and they would be smooching and rolling around on
the couch. Then Nana would start to scream and
when me and Raymond would turn around Nana
would yell at us, "You watch your cartoons and
you don't pay attention to us." The next thing we
knew they were pulling down their pants and stuff.
Then the screaming really started. Sometimes me
and Raymond would run out of the house. But then
Raymond would stand on the porch and peek in the
windows. Then he would tell me the most disgusting
things I have ever heard.

I think this was going on a long time because Nana
and her boyfriends would talk about things they did
before I was even born. They talked about Bakersfield
a lot. Nana used to tell us how pretty she was when
she was young. And I would say, "Were you as pretty
as Penny?" Then she would get mad.

Only two more weeks until summer. Maybe only
two more weeks to live. I wish I could talk to my
father. I really don't want to die. The moon looks
really cool tonight.

24

From the Diary of
P.A. Thayer—Last Entry

Feb 27 Sunday 1955   *day 58*

I am now living at the South St. Paul Hotel.
My room is hotter than hell!

Feb 28 Monday 1955   *day 59*

Back to work today. Boy what a day. Didn't get home
till 2:15 A.M. And am I tired.

Les has been at the house nearly all the time since I left.
Should pound him into ground but won't.

Kate offered to pay for the divorce when it comes up so
that frees me of that worry. Now if I can get the support
for the kids taken care of in some fashion.

I took Kate $300.00 today to catch up on the bills with

and $7.00 besides. I held out $50 for myself. How ever if she needs more she may have it.

Think I'll go down for a cup of coffee and then retire.

～

March 4 Friday 1955   *day 63*

8:00 P.M. Out last nite. O boy got kind of stiff.

Pay day today. Kate gets $50 and me well I get what's left over if any. However I'm building up a little cash reserve for emergencies etc. I hope my income will stay high enough to stand the strain. I'll get by but how about the kids and Kate?

Wish Freddie would call so I could either retire or go out and tip one or two.

Freddie called at 9:30. Bless her. She is taking care of my kids. Guess I'll go over and sit with her a while.

～

March 5 Sat 1955   *day 64*

Just got home at 1:10 last nite. Got in bed and slept 1 hour when Kate called and got me up. Wanted to talk. So over I went. Didn't get back to bed at all.

Looked for a car this day. No soap.

～

March 6 Sunday 1955   *day 65*

Bought a '49 Olds today. Paid too much for it. Will pick it up tomorrow.

~

March 11 Friday 1955   *day 70*

Bad week I guess. I got my big car. Was out with Freddie several times. Got in fight with Pa Walker.

Freddie moved back to Wisconsin. For which I am very sad. And I worked all week.

~

March 12 Sat 1955   *day 71*

It is now 6:55 A.M. and I am up. Got kind of plastered last nite. Darn it. That's got to stop.

Mom called to see if I was all rite. Told her I would be over this A.M. as I don't work.

Boy this has been a rough week on old Zeke. Think I'll sleep all next week.

I wish people would leave me alone. Every day the phone rings for me. Not so bad but at the most awful times and most of the time I'm not around to answer it. The hotel clerk is going to get mad at me yet.

Well guess I'll clean up a bit and have breakfast and go some place for a while.

March 15 Tues 1955   *day 74*

It has been nice and warm altho a mist has been falling all day.

Well I signed some divorce papers today. Nothing for me to do now but wait.

It will cost me $50 a week till Kate remarries and $20 per week from then on till the kids are 21.

I'll be 50 by that time.

Just another day at work.

25

Steve—Letter to Angela

April 19, 1992   Lake Elmo, Minnesota
Easter Sunday   Misty today

Dear Angela,

My father didn't live to fifty. He died of cancer at the age of forty-nine. He was the epitome of the World War II working man. After the war he left the farm and moved to the cities in search of a job. For twenty years he worked in the freezer of a meat-packing plant, until the plant closed down. Then he went to work for a steel mill, until the steel mill closed down. He took a janitor's job at a downtown office building, until he got laid off. He was unemployed when he died. Your grandfather Zeke lost the first five children he had. All sons. My mother took the first four. God took the fifth. Nice man. Hard life.

In all fairness, my mother never got to tell her side of the story. Who's to know what demons she was running from?

Who's to know what fifty years, five children, and two husbands can do to a woman? All she left behind was a note that she scribbled from her hospital bed, where she had being diagnosed with colon cancer, and liver cancer, and stomach cancer . . .

> *One thing I want you all to know and you probably don't believe it; but the most beautiful part of my life was raising you kids.*

There's not much more to tell. In the final years, divorced from Les, there were no more fights. No more anger. Alcohol had drained her of the energy that anger requires. The last time I saw my mother before she went back into the hospital for the last time, was when I drove her down to the clinic to pick up her medicine. She'd had two major operations in less than a year. I was driving her home from the clinic when she asked me if I could drop her off at the bar. It is one of the last memories I have of your grandmother Kate, hobbling across Old Hudson Road and into the neighborhood bar. Her demons finally caught up with her in 1986.

Your grandfather Les followed her to the grave six months later. A lifetime of smoking finally caught up with him. He died of emphysema and congestive heart failure.

As we go through life, Angel, we make choices . . . and then we must live with the consequences. My parents had to make some difficult choices. Who's to say they chose wrong, or that they'd choose anything different? Please don't think of this as a sad letter. You pass through stages, Angel, and as the years go by, a funny thing happens. All the sad and bitter feelings drift away, and what you're left with are the smiles. When I think about my father today, it brings a smile to my face. What a great guy. Even when I think back on the antics of my crazy mother and my goofy step-father, I smile till I break out laughing. I can see the same thing happening with Penny. Especially when I think of what she left me . . . you!

Why didn't I get a letter from you this week? I called the other night, but Nana said you weren't home. Where were you? Is everything OK?

In the newsroom we've been watching the trial of those policemen who beat up Rodney King. I think they'll be found guilty. Don't you? If they're not, all hell could break loose out there. You be careful.

Look up *epitome* for me. And write!

I love you, Angel. Counting down the days now. See you soon.

Steve

26

Miss Crist—Letter to Steve

May 18, 1992
Los Angeles, Calif.

Dear Steve,

My name is Doria Crist. I live across the street from your daughter, Angela. She is one of my favorite little people. Angela introduced us once, just briefly. As you may or may not remember, I am semi-retired. I teach high school part-time here in Los Angeles.

I am writing to you out of concern for your daughter. I believe that Angela is in an abusive situation that is growing increasingly worse.

On the evening of April 17, I was watering plants at my front window when I saw Angela come running out of her house. She was in hysterics. I could see blood running from her nose. She raced down the stairs crying, and began running

down the street. At first I thought that she had been fighting
with her cousin again, until I saw Raymond standing up the
street watching all of this. Then Angela's grandmother came
rushing out the door. She was furious. Like most people in the
neighborhood, I only know her as "Nana." She chased Angela
down the street and caught up with her at the end of the block.
What happened next could only be described as a beating.
When Nana was done beating on her she began dragging Angela home by her hair. I come from the old school of discipline,
but this was not discipline. This was abuse. At that point I ran
out of the house and confronted Nana on the sidewalk. I told
her that I had called the police. Angela was sent into the house
while Nana and I staged a scene outside.

Then I went home and I really did call the police. They
showed up about an hour later. This is a predominantly black
neighborhood. The Los Angeles police aren't much help here.
Although they basically did nothing, they did take a report.

I do not presume to know what your story is, why your
daughter lives with her grandparents here in Los Angeles. I do
know that your wife died when Angela was a baby (I'm very
sorry), but other than that I know very little about you. But
from my front window I have seen the two of you together on
your visits. I've seen how Angela lights up in her father's pres-
ence. I've seen the smile she brings to your face.

But her smile is gone. Now Angela runs home from school
every day—I should say *sprints* home from school every day.
After that, she's never seen until she leaves for school the next
morning. I suspect she's grounded. It breaks my heart watching
her run up the street to that house. The life seems drained from
her face, and she is a little girl so full of life. I hope you don't
think I'm just a nosey neighbor. I like to think I'm a concerned

neighbor. Things were different in my day. Families were strong, and so were the neighborhoods.

I just wanted you to know what's going on here. Please call or write if I can be of any help.

Sincerely,

Doria Crist

27

Angela's Diary

It Is Memorial Day
May 25, 1992
at 11 P.M.

There was only one week left before summer
vacation. Even school, which I like, was getting very
sad for me because everybody was excited about
summer. But I was still grounded and <u>That Woman!</u>
had canceled my vacation to Minnesota for no
reason. I had no contact with my father for weeks.
He called a couple of times, but Nana told him I was
not at home. Then he stopped calling.

Last Friday the last bell rang and I had fifteen
minutes to get my little green eyes home or else. It
wasn't easy running all that way. I grabbed my books
and I hurried through the hallways. They were
crowded. I went out the front door of the school and

ran down the steps as fast as my legs would carry
me. Then I ran to the corner. I didn't even have time
to stop and talk to my girlfriends. Some of the boys,
mostly Raymond's friends, made fun of me as I ran
by them. They knew I had to get home fast or Nana
would beat my butt.

The sun was shining bright. But that only made
me more sad. It looked like a great day to play. I ran
to the corner and waited for the light to change. It is
a really busy street and we have to cross with the
light because a couple of years ago a girl got hit by a
car and was killed when she crossed against the
light. The light takes a long time to change. So I was
just standing there waiting while the afternoon sun
was shining in my eyes.

I noticed a man across the street. He was wearing
sunglasses, but it looked like he was staring at me.
The cars kept going by so I kept losing sight of him.
But every time the traffic cleared there he was
watching me. So I looked away trying to ignore him.
A stinky bus went by, then the light finally changed
and the walk signal came on. I started to walk across
the street. The man was still looking at me. Then the
most powerful feeling came over me, like I'm not
sure if it was a feeling of fear or happiness. Maybe
it was a little bit of both. As I started across the
street I had the feeling that the man was maybe my
father. I hadn't seen him in almost a year. When I
was about halfway across the street he took off his
sunglasses and a big smile came across his face. I
dropped my books right in the middle of the busy

street and I ran with tears in my eyes and I jumped
into the open arms of my father.

I couldn't talk or anything because I was crying so
hard. He didn't talk either. He just held me tight. All
the other kids were walking by staring at us. Elana
Pedilla picked up my books in the street and carried
them over to me.

"Angela, you dropped your books."

"Thank you," I said to her, but with one hand I
was still clinging to my father.

Some of the boys came by and I heard them say,
"That's her father because her father is a white
man." It wasn't disrespectful or anything.

I didn't see Raymond anywhere and I was glad
because he would have told Nana and ruined my
father's secret plan.

We walked to the car with him holding my hand.
We still weren't talking mostly because I couldn't
stop crying. He drove us to McDonald's and bought
me a Coke at the drive-thru. The Coke tasted really
good and helped me get my wits back. I stopped
crying. There were red roses in the backseat. At first
I thought they were for me. We were driving down
Whittier away from Nana and Grandpa's house.

"Where are we going?" I asked.

"I thought we'd go see your mother," he said.

We turned off of the street and into the cemetery.
It was very green and very peaceful. The trees were
tall and provided lots of shade from the sun. Pink
and white blossoms were in bloom. I think we were
the only ones in the whole cemetery. My father got
the flowers from the backseat and handed them to

me. Then we walked up to my mother's grave, right next to where my uncle James is buried.

It is a rose-colored stone on the side of a small hill. It reads PENNY in big letters. A single rose is carved in the stone. It tells the year that she was born, 1958, and the year that she died, 1982. Below the dates are carved these words, "She died like a rose, young and beautiful."

The roses were bundled together with a string. My father took out his trusty pocketknife with the yellow handle and cut the string. Then I laid the fresh roses down on the grave of the mother that I never knew. We made an arrangement with the flowers. Then me and my father bowed our heads in a silent prayer. I started to cry again.

My father wiped a tear from his own eyes then he got down on one knee in front of me. He took out a handkerchief and wiped away my tears. Then he wiped my nose.

"Angel," he said, "there are things I've never told you because I thought you were too young to understand . . . but you're almost ten years old now and I think maybe the time has come. I was planning to tell you this summer anyway . . . I've been trying to tell you in my letters . . ."

My father was having a real hard time talking, because he's not much of a talker. He says that's why he writes. He would look down at the ground. He would glance over at the gravestone. Then he would look up at me.

"When Penny went into the hospital the last time," he explained, "Nana came over to the house and took

you away. I can't remember if I asked her to, or not.
She was just being a good grandmother. The thing of
it is . . . I kind of forgot about you. And when Penny
died . . . I just didn't want to think about you. I knew
you were safe with Nana and Grandpa, so I ran back
to Minnesota . . . and I just kind of forgot about you.
I mean . . . I didn't even stop at the house to say
goodbye . . . or hold you . . . or kiss you. The only
excuse I have is that I was so sad after Penny
died . . . I wasn't thinking. I certainly wasn't
thinking about you. For years I pretended that Los
Angeles was just a bad dream I had once. It's only as
the years went by that I began to remember that I
had a daughter, and what a lousy father I was being.
I thought about my own father and everything he
meant to me. At first I believed that sending money
would somehow make up for it . . . and then maybe
coming to see you on holidays. Now I realize there is
no making up for what I did to you."

He looked over at the gravestone again because
there were tears forming in his eyes. Then he turned
back to me.

"Penny made me promise her that I wouldn't let
you end up with Nana. I broke that promise."

I didn't think he was going to be able to finish
what he had to say. And I didn't care, because I
wasn't really liking what he was telling me. But then
he went on.

"I came out here today to apologize to you for the
past ten years . . . to ask for your forgiveness . . .
and if you can find it in your heart to forgive me . . .
to ask if would you like to come back to Minnesota

and live with me . . . be a daughter to me . . . and let me try to be a real father to you?"

I saw an old Bette Davis movie once. It was so old it was in black and white. She said in the movie that if you love somebody, you can forgive anything. What he said was everything that I ever wanted to hear. I knew that someday he would come and straighten everything out. That someday I would live with my father. I told him, "I know how much it must have hurt when Penny died. I forgive you . . . and I'd like to come and live with you in Minnesota . . . if that's possible."

Of course I was thinking of what Nana would say and do.

But he smiled when I said that, even though I saw a tear roll down his face.

"You didn't do anything wrong, Angel. Nana was never going to let you spend this summer with me. Because she knew in her heart you would never come back. Nana is a woman who doesn't know how to let go."

"When would we leave?" I asked him.

"Right now, with just the clothes on your back. The plane takes off at six-thirty. I have tickets for two. With traffic, we're going to have to hurry. By the time Nana gets around to calling the police, you'll be in Lake Elmo."

"Will we ever come back here to visit?"

"Yes, but it will be a long time from now."

I knew that I wanted to go more than anything in the whole world. But for just a minute standing at my mother's grave I couldn't help thinking about

Grandpa and Nana, and even about Raymond. I love them all very much. I thought about the house up on the hill where my mother grew up and about the same room that we shared. About how we watched different riots from the same window. I thought about my friends and my toys and about Miss Crist across the street. It was hard to believe that I was leaving them all behind, probably for good. But I belonged with my father. And I know how this sounds terribly vain but looking into his eyes that day, I thought that he needed me even more than I needed him. So in the end I saw to it that he kept the promise that he made to Penny so many years ago.

"We'd better hurry," I told him, "or we're going to miss our plane."

When I said that we hugged each other tight. Then he stood. "Say goodbye to your mother," he told me.

I turned to the rose colored stone. I was crying again. I gave a weak wave. "Goodbye, Penny. We'll be in Minnesota."

Today is Memorial Day. Me and my father went to Fort Snelling National Cemetery and we brought flowers to the graves of my grandfather Zeke. To my grandmother Kate. And to my grandfather Les. Then tonight for the first time I stood in the bay windows with my father and watched the moon come up over Lake Elmo.

It's late now. To bed with me.

28

Steve—Letter to Miss Crist

June 7, 1992   Lake Elmo, Minnesota

Dear Miss Crist,

Ask me what's wrong with America, and I will tell you . . . it is the absence of the American father. Ten years ago I did the most cowardly thing a man can do: I deserted my child. I suppose the fact that Angela was black made the decision easier. I assure you, Miss Crist, I was not raised that way. For all of their problems, and they had many, my parents were good people. I could spend this entire letter trying to explain my behavior, but they would only be feeble excuses for what is at heart inexcusable.

My grand plan to win back my daughter was to bring her to Minnesota this year in the guise of a summer vacation. Once here, she would fall in live with the land, and she would stay. But your letter convinced me that I could not afford to wait until summer. Nana was never going to let

Angela go. I guess I always knew that. So I flew to Los Angeles last month and picked up my daughter after school. I gambled that after the fight with you, Nana would be reluctant to call the police and report Angela missing. I was right. As soon as we reached Lake Elmo, I called your local precinct to let them know that I had taken custody of Angela. They still hadn't heard from Nana. We owe you a lot. Thank you.

When things settle down and everybody cools off, I'll work out some kind of deal with Nana. Try to compensate her monthly for the ten years that she raised my daughter. That woman raised two beautiful girls. She just couldn't hang on to them, that's all.

I don't expect Angela to be returning to Los Angeles for a long time. But I want her to maintain a loving relationship with her grandparents. It's important because my own mother and father are gone. All that I can tell Angela of her grandparents on my side of the family are stories . . . a seemingly endless supply of wonderful stories, but still they're only stories. My father grew up on a farm in Wisconsin during the Great Depression. My daughter watched the Los Angeles riots from her bedroom window. Three generations of an American family.

I have a couple of unopened letters here. One of them was written by my father in the Philippines during WWII. It's dated Feb 5, 1945. It was rejected by navy censors and returned to him . . . I don't believe they were allowed to write about combat. The sealed envelope was among my stepmother's papers when she died. I haven't yet had the heart to open it. The other letter is addressed to Angela. It's from her mother. Penny wrote the letter barely a week before she died. It too is sealed, and I have no idea what it says. Penny asked me to give it to Angela on her wedding day. It might be nice to open my father's letter that same day.

Angela is in summer school now, making new friends and trying to make up for lost time. She'll start public school in the fall, one of those all-white schools so prevalent here in the suburbs of the Midwest. My daughter will be one of those two black kids that I used to pass in the halls once a week.

You were a good neighbor, Miss Crist. Angela talks about you often. She'll be writing you soon. As a schoolteacher, you've had a lifetime of children. I've had less than a month. In his diary, my father once wrote, "I've a challenge to meet. I wonder if I can meet it? What foolish talk. Of course I can meet it. I know I can."

Now his son has a challenge to meet. Hopefully in another ten years I'll have Angela all grown-up. Educated, happy, and out on her own. I'll be fifty by then.

Please stay in touch with us. And thank you again for your help.

Steve

They are not long, the days of wine and roses . . .
                                    —Ernest Dowson
                                      (1896)

EPILOGUE
Penny—Letter to Angela

Hi, Angela   11/12/82

I bet you never thought you would hear from me! I hope this letter doesn't freak you out. Mostly I just want you to know how really proud I am to be your mother. I really hope you're happy. (Are you?)

I remember my wedding. It was just me and Steven. He bought me a wedding ring with money he didn't have. You don't realize how much it meant to me. That was the nicest thing anyone has ever given me. Someday it will belong to you. We got married on Catalina Island and had our honeymoon there. I wish you could have seen the beautiful view from our room. I know you would love it.

I hope your father started dating and giving love a try. Or did once again his stubbornness win out? He really shouldn't spend his time thinking about the past so much.

Things are not going so well for me. I'm having more problems than I can handle but I know it will be over soon. Since this happened times are hard but I'll get to heaven a stronger person. I would send you a picture with this letter but you wouldn't know me. All this worrying has aged me. I look like hell!

I'm sorry, this should be a happy cheerful letter with good news, great advice, and all that. But it's just a letter. I shouldn't be telling you all my problems. I do thank God for what I have. It's just that I still haven't learned why it is that I have to die so young. I wanted so much to hold my own and maybe find a career. (And I'm really sorry that I couldn't be there for you!)

Steven and I just had a big fight. He's mad because I'm dying. I'm worried what he'll do when I'm gone. Did he take you back to Minnesota? I hope so. Los Angeles is a city of nuts and fools. When I came home from the hospital and found you were living at Nana's house, all hell broke loose. I don't want you with that woman. I made him promise to raise you. I'll haunt that sucker if he didn't.

I would always joke with your father about blacks not being in Minnesota. I think someone told me that. When he first told his family about me, he told them that I was a dark-haired beauty with big brown eyes. I don't think they got it. (I'm laughing.) It sounds like he's going to have to break our marriage secret to the people in Minnesota. I would love to see his mother's face when she sees you.

I still remember the things Steven would tell me about his mother and his stepfather. I hope he tells you the same stories. I still laugh when I think about the things he would tell me.

Oh little Angela, I'm stuck in this bed and I'm going crazy. I want to go to the beach, put on my skates, and cruise all around. I want to drive a white Corvette down Sunset Boulevard. I want to go to Paris and sit at a sidewalk café. I want to hold my baby in my arms and rock her to sleep. Will someday you do all those things for me?

With all this time in bed I'm doing a lot more reading. I'd hoped to be reading your father's novel soon. My hopes are very high for him and his book. I'm keeping my fingers crossed. I'll say a prayer. (I hope it sells.)

It's hard to imagine my little baby all grown up. When you read this, you might even be older than me when I wrote this. Wouldn't that be something.

I hope you're happy, Angela. I sure was.

I'm going to say good-bye now. Until I see you in heaven, take care of yourself. And take care of your father.

I love you very much.

Your mother,

Penny

AFTERWORD
Steve—Letter to His Father

June 19, 2000
Just past midnight

Edina, Minnesota
Rainy and cool

Dear Dad,

Several years ago, while being treated for depression, I was asked to write you a letter. I reminded the shrink that you'd been dead for twenty years, and that you probably wouldn't read it, but he said that wasn't the point . . . write it anyway. I tried, but after several false starts I discovered it was a lot easier to write fictional letters to my fictional daughter than it was to write a real letter to my dead father. Funny thing happened then . . . my fictional daughter began writing back. So I took my letters to her, and her letters to me, threw in your diary from 1955, and came up with a short novel about fatherhood at the end of the twentieth century. I titled it: *Moon over Lake Elmo*.

I hope you're not too upset. I'm sure anyone who reads

the diary can see that it was never meant to be read by anybody but you . . . and that it was never meant to hurt anybody. As I write this, few people even know the diary exists. But I am forever haunted by that one line you wrote, about not wanting all of your thoughts to pass into oblivion. So with some sleight of hand, I got your diary published. I edited it some, because you tended to ramble on (sorry), but I didn't change anything, or add anything.

Also, Uncle Harvey passed on some of your letters home from World War II. You'll be proud to know there's a renewed interest in the veterans of World War II, especially among young people. I was out at Fort Snelling on Memorial Day. There were traffic jams getting in and out of the cemetery. You and Bret lie under a cluster of trees that get taller and taller every year. Makes you easy to find.

Well, Dad, I want to keep this short . . . it's late. I used to write until the sun came up. I can't do that anymore. It wasn't healthy. Sometimes, typing under the lamplight late at night, I look at the backs of my hands, and I see the hands of an old man. It scares me. Think about it . . . in just two years, I'll be older than you were when you died. Won't that be something.

Still too many cloudy days. Still searching for the sun.

I miss you.

Steve